A Smile Takes Life

A Smile Takes Life

Sundara The Prostitute

Darshan

PARTRIDGE

To order additional copies of this book, contact
Partridge India
000 800 10062 62
orders.india@partridgepublishing.com

www.partridgepublishing.com/india

Contents

Acknowledgement

It is my rhapsody to handover my debut creative adventure in the realm of short story writing to my unknown and enthusiastic readers whose appreciation, warm and titanic positive reception to literary creations have created many charismatic literary personalities who brought never ceasing, ending, fading glory and hallow to the world of English literature. The writer exists and gets immortalized just because of the existence of the appreciative readers who taste his creative feast and spread it's fragrance to the generations. My adventure is just like that of a little kid who tries to acquire the knave of taking step with the admiring and motivating support of his father who is his audience and who appreciates his every step and makes him walk on his feet in the quickly walking world. It is my sweet optimism that my audience and my readers would give their helping hand and would enable me to walk in the vast universe of literature and ignite my sweet hope eventually to reach up to that literary horizon where every writer wants to rest.

I really experience the dearth of words to express my sincerest feel of thanks to "Partridge India" who first offered me that helping hand which kept my literary spirit alive and enabled me to walk with my own literary emotions and add my own literary fragrance to ever blooming lotus of English literature. My dream to be a writer would have been a dream only seen and forgotten if this topmost and widely honored publication could not have rendered its helping hand. I am really very thankful to "Partridge India" and its entire editorial team who trusted my literary competence and imagination and rendered me a golden opportunity to unveil my literary face in their great literary mirror.

My journey of creative writing has just incepted and it has long to go ceaselessly. When I was about to board the train bound to remarkable and rapturous destinations in the world of literature and creative writing, I had a turn back at the platform and I got astonished to see so many visages bidding farewell and with thumbs up gestures, inspiring and supporting smile wishing me dreamed success in my journey to the world of Literature. Some visages were very striking to whom I could not afford to un-notice and there were many among the crowd whose appearance was somewhat invisible to my grateful eyes. Their presence is ever recorded with inspiring voice at every turn of my life. I would like to take the note of such striking and ever present faces that wish my journey and pray for its literary success.

There are some significant people who contributed a lot to my professional career. The first and the foremost among them is Hon. Shri. Ravindraji Mane, former Minister of the State of Maharashtra and the Chairman of Probodhan Shikshan Prasarak Sanstha (PSPS), Ambav, Devrukh, Ratnagiri Maharashtra and Mrs. Neha Mane his better half who are responsible for my bread and butter. I always feel in their debt as they gave me their helping hand in my adverse and discouraging circumstances. They offered me a hope to stand and continue my life in criticalities.

There are some people who have given their outstanding contribution to my academic achievements. The first and the foremost is Dr. Chauhan A. S., Ph.D. guide of Rashtrasant Tukdoji Maharaj University, Nagpur whose valuable contribution made my Ph.D. submission possible. I am also thankful to Ramesh Belsare, an official in Ph.D. Cell, Rashtrasant Tukdoji Maharaj University, Nagpur who gave me his helping hand during my entire Ph.D. process.

My family has been a vital force in my literary journey. Ceaseless inspiration of my loving departed father Late. Ishwar Naroba Wakde who taught me the lessons of innocence, honesty, dedication and devotion and always wanted me to be different from him. My mother Mrs. Parvati Ishwar Wakde who always wishes to see her son standing quite high in the esteem of the world always supports me in my adventure and never let me get disheartened in my courage stealing and frustration inculcating blows of the destiny. Her love and care energies and revitalizes my every step towards adventures. I always feel rather lucky guy to have very supporting, encouraging and understandable wife Mrs. Asha Wakde whose presence at every literary discussion gives me creative acceleration and new vision of diverse and unknown literary ideas. She is always ready with her helping hand whenever and wherever she finds me to be tumbling in gyre of criticalities of life. Without her, the work would have been just a seen but never fulfilled dream. I am very thankful to my loving kids Aryan and Rajveer Balasaheb Wakde who deprived themselves from fatherly love, affection and care as I could not spare time for them being engaged in my work. There are some other family members who are always ready with their thumbs up gestures to my mission in life to whom I am grateful are my elder brother Mr. Laxman Ishwar Wakde his entire family and my loving and caring sister Mrs. Aruna Balaji Bhoite.

Eventually there are some friendly faces to whom I cannot afford to ignore in my feel of gratitude. The first and foremost is my friend Ms. Darshana Salvi who is the most respectable, estimable and adorable professional colleague and personal friend of mine with whom I always have Literary Discourse. She is a great well-wisher of mine and an emotional support in my professional career and personal life. She supports me in every creative work and acts like a ceaseless fountain of inspiration and courage which enables me to enjoy my life with all its roughs and smoothes.

My chummy Mr. Sominath Mitkari has been a very vital support during the process of writing this book and other creative endeavors. He gave me very worth welcoming suggestions which proved to be very vital in writing this book. Prof. Ashok Jadhav and Prof. Shivnarayan Waghmare, close friends of mine, gave a very significant contribution during manuscript correction process.

Mr. Rajesh Jadhav, Dr. Sudarshan Awasthi, Mr. Kishore Khatane, Mr. Sandip Kotwal, Mr. Suresh Indulkar and his family, Mr. Vayakos V.K., Mr. Patel S. D. and Ms. Ashwini Swami are some of the friendly faces in the never ending queue of well-wishers to my literary and creative journey to whom I pay my sincerest thanks for their love, affection and care.

Review

1. **Madhumati**: A girl named Madhumati from a poor family aspiring for education falls in love with his History Professor and gets married with him without bothering what the world will think of her relation with him. She has been cherishing desire to see Tajmahal which her husband fulfills. But when the couple is about to enter Tajmahal, Madhumati misses her purse at the tea stall where they had tea. For this, she has to cross the road. While crossing the road a heavily loaded truck crushes her and the Professor goes mad ultimately dies jumping down from the Tajmahal.

2. **Sundara the Prostitute**: How setbacks in the personal life of a housewife Mrs. Sundara Murthy transform her into a strumpet and her good deeds for the sake of an earthquake affected place transform her into a spiritual personality is the focus of the story.

3. **Divided Love:** Differentiating treatment of the Parents towards their sons leads the family on the verge of destruction. When the first son is born in the family he becomes the apple of the eyes of the Parents. He becomes the first priority but with the arrival of the second, the

first one is neglected. The ignoring treatment leads the first son on the wrong path which brings a lot of defame to the family. To save further defame, the Parents confine him in a dark room. Now the second becomes their darling doing everything for his sake. One day the confined son succeeds in running away and he emerges as a great building contractor. The second son takes the examination of the final year of M.B.B.S. and on the day of result he is caught in an accident. The family gets collapsed with the second son's death. Fully frustrated family leaves their native reaches to Pune to join an NGO. Luckily they meet their first son in a hotel. He requests them to stay with him in his home but the parents deny the offer.

4. **A Flower of Wisdom**: A college student trying to molest a girl gets in ambush with his college Professor. The event has such an adverse impact on the Professor that he commits suicide. The accused student gets lifelong imprisonment for his misdeeds. The darkness and unbearable confinements of the jail and the people he meets there transform him into a through philanthropist who cultivates a nursery in the jail and whatever the earning he gets from his nursery business, he sends it to his Professor's affected family. Because of his help, the family gets settled and the son becomes a doctor. When the doctor, the son of the murdered Professor, comes to know about the help of murderer of his father, he brings him home treats and serves him like a fatherly person.

5. **Success:** An ordinary writer writes for the local news paper contributing to all forms of literature and using earning coming out of it to overcome the financial worries of the family. He is blessed with ever decaying house of the ancestors and an ever ailing mother who corrodes him inwardly. The happiest thing for him in all these miserable conditions is his status as a writer. When someone comes calling him as a writer he feels proud of it and his wife also. Both the writer and his wife are hopeful that one day or the other writer's writing genius would create a classic which would overcome their financial problems. The worries trouble him a lot. The writer falls ill and during that period he writes a novel named *'Success'*. The novel ends and with that ends the life of the Writer. The novel is by chance published and proves to be classic bringing a lot of fame, name recognition and prosperity to the family. His wife starts publishing house in his memory to offer a chance to many hidden writers. As a result wonderful pieces of literary works are created and literature enjoys renaissance after a dark period.

6. **Essence of Life:** A successful jeweler hates books for whom reading books and taking education is a worthless activity. He thinks that it directs one's life in no way. He believes that the true knowledge comes from experience and not from books. He hates the books and does not let his children complete his education and asks them to handle his jewelry business.

One day he falls ill and gets frustrated with treatment meted out to him by his family members. Accidently, he reads a book turns out to be a true lover of books and opens libraries all over the nation.

7. **Dead Fish:** A farmer's son whose father has been murdered by a Politician by forcefully pouring poisonous wine into his mouth takes revenge of the Politician in the same way using fish as an agent of revenge

8. **Life Survived and Death Postponed**: Cotton like Puppy whose mother is poisoned by the Nagar Panchayat goes out and gets separated from other puppies. In search of his mother he enters a bungalow where he meets his new mistress, Rupa. Very soon he succeeds in making a separate place for himself in the house of Rupa. He loves all and all the members of the family love him. Playing with Rupa is a great pastime for him. One day the confined Puppy goes out of the bungalow when his mistress is chasing him in a hide and seek game, suddenly he comes under a vehicle but luckily gets escaped.

9. **A Smile Takes Life**: A beggar is ill-treated by the Landlord in the town when the beggar visits his edifice. A beggar feels very sorry at the insulting treatment at the hand of the Landlord. During the course of the time the Landlord's life gets engaged in severe setbacks which he cannot overcome. His family is perished and he becomes a poor Landlord living in a rented room in the town. One day

the beggar who is in the habit of taking lottery tickets wins a lottery. He builds the same kind of edifice which the Landlord had. One day the poor Landlord is having a walk in the town and suddenly his eyes catch an edifice like him. Out of curiosity he visits it and peeps through the half open gate at that time the beggar transformed rich man is busy in washing his car. When their eyes meet the beggar turned rich man gives him a smirk and it makes the poor Landlord broken at heart. He returns home and ends his life.

10. **The School for the Thieves**: A thief is about to enter another thief's house with the intention of the theft. But there comes Police and he hides himself behind the wall and peeps through the window. He gets shocked to hear the conversation that the thief in the house has been brutally killed by the angry mob. When the wife of the murdered thief hears it, she falls dead. The small boy is crying over the abrupt happenings. The Police depart and the thief enters the house picks up the boy and educates him. In the course of the time the boy emerges as a great education institute owner who prohibits the entry of the children of the socially black listed people in his educational institute. The thief gets hurt by his son's (boy's) behaviour. He tries to convince his son but he fails. He leaves him and starts a school for such children named '*The School for the Thieves*'

11. **As You Sow, So You Reap:** Fully frustrated doctor with his unsuccessful medical practice

becomes the richest doctor in the town overnight by playing with the lives of so many people to whom he injects drugs. He realizes the severity of his deeds when his own son becomes the victim of drug addict.

12. **Horoscopes**: It is a story of a son of a peasant's family which has never seen prosperity for generations. When baby boy is born in the family, the mother goes to horoscope maker to make a horoscope of her newly born son. She gets disappointed when she comes to know that her son has no future. His mother makes two horoscopes for self satisfaction when the horoscope predicts future for her son: one showing dark future and the second showing bright. The son gets two horoscopes at two different points of time in his life. He begins his life with the horoscope showing dark future for him and the impact of this horoscope is so much that he becomes a victim of it and goes astray. Accidently, the second horoscope falls in his hand showing bright future for him and he gets confused with a question how a person can have two horoscopes. For some times, he keeps the first horoscope aside and acts on the second which predicts that he would be a successful businessman. Accordingly, he becomes so. One day after becoming a successful businessman he takes out both the horoscopes and goes to the horoscope maker who made it. He tells the truth behind that and he tells him the secret of his success that it is not horoscope but his attitude which made him successful.

13. **Red Inspiration:** Once, a doctor's son falls ill. Doctor does all that that is possible to make him fit but all efforts go in-vain. A visitor brings a rose for him. The sick boy consistently stares at the rose. It's every dropping petal teaches him lessons of life and gets him cured. What hurts him is not the death of the rose but its fragmented death. He wants that it should be complete. He grows, takes education and becomes a Botanist. He makes research and finds out such liquid when it is injected in the flowers, the flowers remain ever fresh and its petals remain intact. He gives the flower a complete death.

14. **Penance:** During a woman's heart surgery, the fingers of the doctor betray him and consequently the woman dies who has a fatherless son. Doctor feels very sad over his mistake and decides to take a penance. He adopts the boy and educates him. For the sake of the boy, the doctor never marries in his life. The son settles down in some city with his wife. When the boy comes to know that his father is suffering from a severe disease, the couple avoids having contact with him. Doctor dies an unnoticed death in waiting to have final meet of his son.

15. **Shortening Life and Growing Concerns**: A farmer whose much of life is spent in serving his parents and then his daughters never gets a chance to lead life for himself and for the sake of his wife who lives her life limiting her needs for the betterment of her family. When

the worries of the family come to an end, the life gets shortened. When the moment comes to enjoy life, life betrays him.

16. **Disgraced Innocence**: Ramdas the head security of an ancient temple has been giving his sincerest service to the temple. One day the golden pinnacle of the temple is stolen away when he is on the duty. He is charged of having hand in the theft and ill treated by the people for the wrong doing. He is boycotted by the town and has to leave the place for his no fault. After the period of twenty or more years the golden pinnacle is recovered and disgraced Ramdas is brought back home and honored with the service in the temple. But before he joins the temple he pays the debt of the Nature.

17. **Masterpiece:** A painter aspiring to create a masterpiece of his career to be sent for an art gallery in France becomes the victim of severe physical ailment and his dream remains incomplete for some time. His son whose body carries painting blood of his father decides to fulfill this dream unfulfilled. With the guidance of his paralyzed father, he succeeds in completing the painting which is declared as the masterpiece of the year by Art Gallery in France.

About the Author

The reader is always hungry for new themes and new ideas never dealt with before. He wants such stories which would give him a greater understanding of human life and it's brighter and darker aspect. He wants such reading which would add a new dimension to his life and would give him courage to face challenges and hardships which are part and parcel of human life and teaches him to keep his feet on the ground if scintillating success comes in his ways. True readers are always in search of moral teaching from the reading. Short stories have always been a good moral teacher enhancing the moral approach of the generations. Majority of the readers prefer the reading of short stories for it gives them pure delight. The present work fulfills all the literary, aesthetic and moral expectations of the readers. That is the reason why the reader will prefer this book.

About the Book/Overview

The book deals with variety of themes. The most appreciable thing about the themes is that the themes are quite new and make the readers feel that they are connected to their lives. The ideas are put in such way that it makes the reader feel that whatever happens in the lives of the characters resemble somewhere to his life. Most of the stories are tragic in nature and on reading the tragedies of the characters, the readers are bound to be moved. The book provides new reading experience to the readers. Emotions dealt with are so powerful that they compel the reader to read the book from the beginning till the end. Some stories carry suspense and to understand it, the reader has to wait till the end of the stories. Unexpected happenings, games of destiny, human errors committed unknowingly, failure and final demolition of the characters and sudden rise in the lives of the characters attract the readers towards the book. The stories are so novel that every reader who has a feel for reading and whose favorite genre is short stories would read this book without fail.

Biographical Information

Mr. Balasaheb Ishwar Wakde has been working as a lecturer in English at Rajenrda Mane Polytechnic, Ambav Devrukh a small place in Konkan Region of Maharashtra since 2010. During his fourteen years service, he gave his valuable teaching contribution to the most reputed Educational Institutes such as Rayat Shikshan Sanstha, Satara, Symbiosis Center for Distance Learning, Pune and other renowned educational institutes. Working with Symbiosis Center for Distance Learning provided him the idea to write and offered him a unique opportunity to act as a co-author. He contributed as a co-author to four books such as Advanced Concepts in Technical Communication, Introduction to Technical Communication and Information Development Life Cycle. He has published papers on Indian English Literature in National Level Research Magazines. He has given his sincerest contribution to one day National Level Seminars on the themes related to English Literature by presenting his scholarly research papers. He had had an opportunity to conduct Training Sessions on Business Communication and Communication Skills for employees of Wipro Call Center, Mumbai and to the employees of John Deere Pvt. Ltd. Pune.

Madhumati

It is one of the hot days in summer. The dark night is taking the reins from the departing dusk and preparing itself to continue the never ending cycle of the nature. The blowing wind is also on duty but it seems that he is grown somewhat sluggish in acceleration of his work and making people restless with troublesome sweat. The lethargic approach of the blowing wind has not only made the surrounding hot but also the lives of people living in. So, most of the people prefer to be out of their hot nests taking shelter under the open umbrella of the sky. It is the time when electricity is yet to reach in the most of the towns and villages in India. Midnapur is one of such villages gradually transforming into a town and yet untouched by the existence of electricity. It is in one of the lanes in Midnapur which ends with a small sized dark wooden house and in its front yard a lantern is burning proudly conveying its existence in darkness. It is under the dying light of the lantern, a girl is dreaming of her tomorrow by burying herself in the world of the book. It is the book of history of the tenth standard and the girl who is reading the book is Madhumati as the loud calling of her mother gives the hint of her name.

While reading the book, she is forced to take a long pause at a chapter which tells the love story of a great Mughal King Shahjahan. On the left page of the book there is a picture of this legendry Mughal King who immortalized himself through his love story and on the right page there is snow like picture of Tajmahal. She starts reading and imagining the lives of the lovers written in black and white and gets engrossed in the mesmerizing love story of Shahjahan which has been motivating and ruling the world of love for years. While reading the concluding lines of the story, Madhumati takes a long pause for she gets fascinated by the snow like Tajmahal and its eternal beauty. She gets so impressed by its beauty that for some moments she becomes oblivion of her own existence and becomes one with the love story of Shahjahan and Mumtaz and the symbol of their pure love that is Tajmahal. Suddenly the sound of the bell in the distant temple strikes that it is 12 O' clock and takes out Madhumati from that world of History. She hurriedly finishes the last few lines of the story and takes a departing glance of Tajmahal and determines at this midnight hour that one day or the other; she will visit the symbol of eternal love of Shahjahan and Mumtaz. It is with this midnight determination, she says 'good bye' to the departing hours of the dying night.

Madhumati has been staying in Midnapur for years. Her father has been working as a coolie and supporting and surviving a small family. Madhumati's mother also works as a maid servant washing and cooking in the rich families and trying to contribute in her own way to the needs of the family in its hard times. Madhumati is the only child of the couple and being so, she is dear to their hearts. They treat her as their son and never blame to the destiny for not giving them a son. They give her education which they can afford and never give her any chance to blame them. Madhumati is very happy in all these conditions and really struggles hard to keep the expectations of her parents alive. Her bright success in her matriculation examination assures her parents that they are spending on the worthy child and enhances their expectations without bothering about the expenses on her higher education; they send her to the college to acquire the wings of ambition to take a high flight in the sky and to change the fortune of the family as well.

It is Madhumati's first day in the college. She enters the college with a lot of hopes and a sense of responsibility. The new educational conditions in the college impress her a lot and it becomes an addict for her that she never misses a single lecture. Her industrious and studious temper makes her acquire a good place in the books of her teachers. When her teachers come to know about her poor financial condition, they willingly come forward to help her in all possible ways and motivate her to continue her studies. Thus she completes twelfth and gets admitted in the first year of arts with history as special subject. Everything is going on very smoothly and all are happy as the things happen with them. Madhumati is complacent as she is struggling hard to stand high in the esteem of all and stepping ahead to fulfill the expectation of her parents.

Her college starts and she goes to attend her history lecture. She sits in the class and knowingly or unknowingly gets fascinated towards her history teacher whose history teaching skills impress her a lot. After the lecture, she meets the teacher who might be almost double of her age but has charming and young look. She greets him, "Good Morning Sir. I am

Madhumati and have been the student of this institute for last several years. May I know your name please?" Her teacher curiously answers her question. "Myself Prof. Vishal Babu and have been serving here since long." Madhumati being already impressed gives an outlet to her admiration for her teacher. She tries to please him saying, "Sir, I have been greatly impressed by the way you deal with this most interesting subject." Teacher looking at her and fascination in her eyes completes the formality by expressing his gratitude. "Thank you, Miss. Madhumati."

Gradually, their meetings after lecture increase and with this increase her subject difficulties also. Madhumati's fascination for the Professor gradually takes the form of love. The simple living and her simple beauty charms Prof. Vishal Babu and she begins to think of him and him only. Soon a romantic transformation is observed in their overall conduct. Their gestures, postures and their facial expressions become their means to convey their hidden feelings of love for each other. Their eyes change their colors and grow mischievous. Soon, Madhumati's respect for him as a teacher gets melted and looks towards him as her lover. Prof. Vishal Babu's plight is not different. Prof. Vishal Babu loses his morality and the power of his love overpowers his professional commitments and adherence. His guilty eyes start escaping from the eyes of the society.

Sudden transformation occurred in the body movements of both Madhumati and Prof. Vishal Babu catches the suspecting eyes. The students in their class discuss their clandestine love affair in their absence. Soon it becomes the talk of the town. In the initial days,

Madhumati and Professor think that what is going on between them is not known to the world. Out of this ignorance, they meet at public places such as tea stall, at the bank of the river which flows outside Midnapur and other shopping places. Once it is the birthday of the Madhumati. Professor is aware of it and he wants to give her a gift as a token of his love. He goes to a gift center. He takes a look at almost all the things but none of them succeed in alluring him. He is about to leave the shop suddenly his eyes are caught by a white Tajmahal framed in the glass. Finally he fixes his mind on that and pays the money and returns home. When they meet next time, he offers her that gift. It makes her very happy. She somewhat surprisingly tells him, "Sir, You have made me very happy. I have been cherishing a great fascination for this great wonder of the world which stands for an immortal love story of the Indian Mughal ruler. I wish to tell you that I have been cherishing a strong desire since my school days to see Tajmahal if life offers me a chance" Encouraging her he says, "Why not? Don't worry I will fulfill your long cherished dream and if possible very soon." This encouragement enhances and strengthens her love for the Professor and makes her close her eyes to his other weaknesses. With this gift, their passion to meet enhances and takes their love towards its desired turn.

The Professor realizes that they are being caught by the captivating eyes of the world and one day or the other; it will make the *Tamasha* of their lives. Professor's conscience begins to torture him as he has not told her that he is married and a childless father and being so it is unfair to have such relation with a girl who is his student. Lying on the bed beside his barren wife, he thinks of Madhumati and the 'hide and seek' game he is playing with his wife. He decides that in his next meeting with Madhumati, he would reveal all the things and put curtain on the whole matter as it is not in the interest of the both. He thinks that it would be better if he reveals the things now otherwise it will be late and thing will be out of the hands. One day with his indicative eyes and speaking gestures he passes his message to Madhumati to meet at the isolated bank of the river. As per the indication given by the Professor, Madhumati reaches there. The Professor putting a stone on his heart tells her "See Madhumati, I am a married fellow and have a nice and loving wife. But we don't have children. In such conditions, doing such would be like a hoodwinking to both you and my loving wife. I think we should stop it here otherwise the things will go worse for us." He anticipates that on hearing this argument she would give up his thought but happens contrary. Innocent already drowned Madhumati in his love; she tells him, "If you truly love me then other things do not matter for me. If you are going to accept me as your wife then I am ready to face whatever may be the consequences of my action." Professor realizes that Madhumati has an indomitable will to have him which makes him never to repeat such things which have least consideration for her.

Once they are caught red handed loitering on the isolated bank of the river. The management of the institute where he works asks him for clarification of his deed and warns him of the consequences of what he does. The college writes a letter to the parents of Madhumati informing about her undesirable relation with the Professor. But fortunately or unfortunately the letter is misplaced and the parents of Madhumati remain in dark about Madhumati's love affair. When the water flows over the head, the couple gets awakened and elopes as there is no other way to end the concern. The news of teacher student love affair and their eloping becomes the breaking news of the news paper. The act of the love birds not only damages the reputation of the institute but their families also. When the parents of Madhumati get the wind of this, initially they are not prepared to have trust on their ears. But when they read the news of elopement of their most trusted daughter, they get collapsed. As Madhumati makes her parents suffer with her deeds like that Professor's action makes his childless wife suffer. When she comes to know that her husband has eloped with his student, she does nothing but drowns herself in flood of tears and confines herself in her house for many days.

The Professor and Maduhmati go to Deharadun and get married there. They wish to be back but they are aware of the fact that it would not be in their interest to go back as Midnapur has become extremely hot for them. They loiter here and there visiting this or that place. It continues for the next sixth months. They think that with the departing time, the things will be alright, the people would accept them and they would re-start their life in Midnapur as it was. The Professor spends all that he has during these six months. He gets aware that his bank balance is finishing now and he has an option either to go back to Midnapur or to do some business wherever they are in case if they don't return. The day comes when the Professor comes to the conclusion that they must go back to Midnapur otherwise they would be bankrupt. They return to Midnapur after a period of six months expecting that their families and of course the people of Midnapur would have forgotten their past history and would welcome them again. When they reach Midnapur, they prefer to go on their previous routes deciding that they will be back at the bed of the river after finishing their business.

When Madumati returns home, she gets shocked to see that someone else is staying there. On getting enquired she comes to know that her parents left the house immediately after the incident had taken place. Since then no one knows where they have been. She tries to collect the information of her parents but none helps her in this matter. There Professor visits his house and finds that his house is locked. He enquires to the neighbor about his wife. The neighbor tells him that she left Midnapur one month after the incident. The neighbor hands over him a piece of paper of his wife. The Professor takes the piece of paper which speaks like this. "You have deceived and defamed me. Your misdeed has made me suffer a lot and with this defame it is not easy for me to continue here for a very long time. I am going back to my native and request you not to come there and show me your betrayed face. I don't wish to see it again." The words in the letter hurt him and hiding that pain he moves from there. Then he returns to his college with the thought that the institute would have forgotten his past and let him rejoin the institute. But he gets extremely disappointed when the Head of the institute hands over him the letter of dismissal. He tries to have a talk with his colleagues but they prefer to have distance from him.

Professor realizes that Midnapur has not forgotten their deeds. Both meet at the bed of the river and decide to leave Midnapur permanently. Madhumati gets worried about the way Midnapur received them. Madhumati gives an outlet to her feeling of worry about their future. "Sir, don't you think that we have done a wrong. If you don't get the job, we will be lost." To kill the intensity of her worry and supporting her he says, "Madhumati, I don't think that we have done anything wrong. We have loved and doing love is not a crime. If the society does not accept, it is its problem. For the sake of reluctant society, we cannot stop living. Don't worry everything will be alright soon. Have patience. Keep it always in mind where there is will, there is a way."

Madhumati continues her life somewhat feeling insecure at heart with this borrowed support of the Professor. The couple manages some amount of money by selling the gold they have. They leave Midnapur and finally settle down in Utty. There he tries to get job in the college but when the institute demands his previous experience certificate, he gives up the thought to work and begins private coaching. Madhumati also supports him side by side by doing sewing work. They continue their life in a rented flat. In the course of time, his classes run speedily and earn enough to survive in Utty. Madhumati also earns good through her sewing work and thus their survival worries come to an end and enjoy the life which they desired for.

One day while resting on the bed Professor gives her a pleasant shock and shows her the two tickets booked for Agra. Madhumati gets shocked and exclaims, "Agra, for what! What is going on? Why is this sudden visit for?" Professor reveals his plan to his confused and ignored wife. "Darling! It has been your wish to see Tajmahal and see the time of its fulfillment has come. Get ready, we are leaving Utty for Agra day after tomorrow." It makes her very happy and she begins for preparation. On the decided day they board the train and leave for Agra.

They reach Agra late in the night. They book a room in a lodge where they spend their night. The next morning they take an auto-rickshaw for going to Tajmahal. When they get down from the auto-rickshaw they, especially Madhumati feels overjoyed to see that huge Tajmahal is standing in front of them and seems to her that he is little bending as if he is paying respect to the love of this couple and giving a warm welcome. Madhumati is about to get fainted in happiness but the Professor puts his hand on her shoulder and says "Control as there is a lot to see ahead. Enshrine your excitement for that also."

On the other side of the road in front of Tajmahal, there is a tea stall where they take breakfast. Professor has nice talk with the fellow who runs the tea stall. After having their breakfast, they move towards the Tajmahal for that they have to cross the road. The road is crowded with vehicles and very difficult to find a way through such a crowd. Professor holds Madhumati's hand and crosses the road. They are about to enter Tajmahal suddenly Madhuamati realizes that she has forgotten a carry bag which contains her purse at the tea stall. Suddenly she forcefully escapes her hand from the hold of Professor and hastily and somewhat anxiously tries to cross the road. Professor gets confused and could not understand why she is running. He shouts fearfully "Hey! Madhumati, where are you going? Don't try to cross the road it is hazardous." Before this sound alerts her and he comes to accompany her, she pierces through the crowded road. Within the blinking of the eyes a speedy tempo hits her and runs over her. The hit is so powerful that she dies on the spot. Flood of blood and scattered flesh turns the road red. Professor does not believe his eyes and ceaselessly shouts "Maddhumati." He tries to reach there finding his way through the crowd gathered at the dead body of Madhumati. When he sees her, he sits down almost dead.

The accident gives him such a shock that he loses the equilibrium of mind and sits there watching at the blood and pieces of flesh spread over the road. The gathered crowd collects the dead body of Madhumati sends it to the hospital for further process. The person who runs the tea stall where they had had tea is the eye witness of the mishap. He feels very sad at the misfortune of the couple. He takes him to his stall tries to offer him a glass of water and a cup of tea. But Professor gives no response to his offer. The tea stall runner understands that the gentleman has gone insane. For many months, Professor takes rounds and rounds around the Tajmahal with the hope that one day or the other he would meet his Madhumati. He sits at the tea stall ceaselessly staring at the Tajmahal and busy in talking to himself as if he is having conversation with his Madhumati. When the darkness falls the tea stall gets closed. Professor sits there for a long time and ultimately sleeps there. His appearance gets changed and his clothes become dirty and torn and his hair grow dirty as a lot of dirt gets stored in it. He gets transformed into a typical mad man.

Most of the times he talks to himself and rarely he has a talk with the tea stall runner. He tells him that his Maduhmati has been captivated in the Tajmahal. He wants to free her and take her back to his town but the security outside is his enemy which prevents him from going in. Once he dares to rush into the Tajmahal but the security guards catch him and give him a good beating. Every day he sits at the tea stall staring at the Tajmahal with the hope that one day or the other he would get the chance to go in to see his Madhumati. It is one of the hot days in summer as so there is no rush of the tourists and viewers in the Tajmahal. The security guards have become little lethargic after their lunch. They are sitting under the shade which protects them from the fire vomiting sun. Seeing them fully engaged in talk and somewhat inattentive, the Professor takes the advantage of it and rushes into the Tajmahal. The security gets alert and sees the mad man has encroached into the Tajmahal. With their gun they chase him. The mad Professor reaches at one of the domes of Tajmahal. When he looks down, he finds that Madhumati is calling him down. Suddenly the security reaches there. They are about to catch him, already scarred Professor thinks that instead of falling into the hands of the enemies who prevent him from meeting Madhumati, it would be far better to meet Madhumati who is waiting and calling him down. Instantly he jumps down. Hurriedly somewhat shocked security guards come down to the floor and finds that the mad man has closed his eyes. The dead body of the Professor is brought out. Seeing the tragic end of the Professor, the tea stall runner mutters "True lovers can never live in isolation"

Sundara the Prostitute

The dawn hides her behind the curtain of the past and the day comes on his mission in the town of Harihareshwara. A slow but dying cacophonous sound of a motorcar takes a pause in front of a double storied bungalow. A newly married couple gets down and gets engrossed in shifting their luggage on the second storey of the bungalow named Shree-Prasad. The newly married couple is Mr. Krishna and Mrs. Sundara Murthy. Mr. Krishna works as a supervisor in firecrackers manufacturing company in Harihareshwara. Mrs. Sundara Murty being ill-educated prefers to be happy in her role as a housewife. It is confirmed from the discussion of the couple that Mrs. Sundara had lost her parents in an accident when she was eight years old and it is her poor maternal grandmother who brought her up. It is on their first night, Mr. Krishna who is already obsessed with her beauty comes up with an appreciable remark for her beauty. He admires her saying, "How beautiful you are! How fortunate I am to have such a beautiful wife!" Mrs. Sundara Murty gets blushed by his complements. It makes her feel proud inwardly but pretends to be taken casually saying, "Thank you very much for this encouraging and lovely complement." She too acknowledges that she is very fortunate enough to have such a husband who loves and appreciates her.

Mr. Krishna further admires her and tries to place her on pedestal saying, "Your beauty has mesmerized me. I am slave to you and to your beauty and will be forever." To this, Mrs. Krishna replies by giving a blushed smile.

Mrs. Sundara Murty is like her name. She is woman of a paramount beauty. If anyone casts his eye on her, loses his senses and becomes a slave of her beauty. Women get jealous of her and men get enamored after her. She being new and an unacquainted with Harihareshwara takes time to get spread the fragrance of her heart killing beauty. Slowly the beauty of Mrs. Sundara comes out of the confinements of the house. Mrs. Sundara has to visit several parts of the town such as market for shopping and the bazzar for buying vegetables to run the household. Slowly, Harihareshwara gets entangled into the beautiful but harmless fire of beauty of Mrs. Sundara. Her paramount and senses stealing beauty becomes the talk of the town. Her beauty is such that anyone of any age category adult, young or middle aged or a toothless dying old man gets insane and enshrines an impossible desire to have her. When the fragrance of her beauty crosses the frontiers of Harihareshwara, the curious lovers of her beauty deliberately come to those places to have a look at her beauty from where she goes on spreading the fragrance of her beauty. The people are so mad after her dying beauty that they get ready to die for the sake of a single look of her and her beauty. Evil eye of the world too becomes passionate to enjoy the feast of her beauty by foul or fair ways. Thus the paramount beauty of Mrs. Murty gives new hope and pleasure of life to the people of Harihareshwara and places around it.

Life of this newly married couple begins happily in Harihareshwara. The couple continues their life being happy in their limited income by limiting their needs. Both are happy in whatever they have and they never let their concerns grow by aspiring for more than what they have. Every night before going to bed, the couple thanks the almighty for making them happier than others who never had and have the taste of happiness. Such is the happy and contended life of Mr. Krishna and Mrs. Sundara Murty. It has become a routine of Mrs. Sundara Murty to meet the admiring eyes and eyes having evil intentions but ignoring them she leads her controlled life.

One day at noon, when the life is lost in the dissonant sounds of the machinery busy in making material for firecrackers, accidently caused short-circuit sets the fire-crackers' godown on fire where Mr. Krishna works. Within the twinkling of the eyes, gigantic waves of fire engulf the godown of the firecrackers manufacturing company. Unfortunately, at this moment Mr. Krishna is on a round to make report on the existing stock of the living firecrackers available in the godown. Suddenly the jarring sounds of the bomb blasts hit the eardrums of the labor along with Mr. Krishna present over there and before they understand what happens, the fire engulfs them leaving a heap of coals and coals of dead bodies at the place where there was a huge go-down a few whiles ago. The uncontrolled crowd of people gathers at the spot. Everything is finished before they can do something to rescue the lives. One of the employees of the company identifies the dead body of Mr. Krishna and reports to the management.

The darkness is about to fall, the Sun is seen counting his last breath at the edge of a distant horizon. Mrs. Krishna happily engaged in doing cooking activities simultaneously keeping her eyes on the arrival of her husband. She is so much engrossed in her activities that she never thinks that this darkness of evening will grab the light permanently from her life. A group of employees brings the covered dead body of Mr. Krishna. The door of Mr. Krishna is locked from inside. One of them knocks at the door. Hearing the sound of the knock, Mrs. Krishna hurriedly comes as if she thinks that it is her husband knocking at the door. She gets surprised to see a stranger at the door. The employee introduces himself as, "Hello! Mam!." Before he adds something to his saying Mr. Krishna hurriedly and a little beat chillingly asks him, "Who are you gentleman and what brings you here?" Fully prepared but somewhat serious inwardly introduces him to her. "I am Rangnath Chakrawarthy, a colleague of Mr. Krishna. Before Mrs. Krishna poses any other question he hastily but in serious tone tells the things happened and brings before her the covered dead body of Mr. Krishna. On seeing the dead body of her husband, Mrs. Krishna makes such a wailing sound that the whole world gets lost into her wailing sound. Wailing sound becomes a louder and louder and after reaching to its extreme becomes silent. Dark silence with spreading darkness comes to stay in the dark life of Mrs. Krishna. Funeral ritual is performed and left no ritual to be performed thereafter in the dark life of Mrs. Krishna.

Mrs. Sundara Murthy's battle for survival begins. After the sudden departure of her husband, Sundara prefers to continue her life in Harihareshwara as she doesn't have any strong relative who can look after and support her except her maternal grandmother who is too old to support her financially in these worst days of Sundara. Being ill-educated, she does not have the opportunities to get employed. The pages of the history of the tragedy get turned one after the other. She begins to work as a maid servant in the house of a landlord. Her seductive beauty is her advantage as well as her disadvantage. Her beauty is fascinating enough to change the colors of the eyes of the people. The beauty changes the colors of the eyes and the mind of her master. Once, the master's wife is out of station. Taking advantage of these solitary conditions, the master has the feast of her beauty. She protests but being helpless and slave to the situation, she learns to accept the turns of her life as they come. Her beauty is exposed to be enjoyed. Mrs. Sundara Murty becomes Ms. Sundara, a very popular and notorious whore in Harihareshwara. She becomes notorious among the housewives for she becomes responsible for spoiling the matrimonial lives of women whose husbands get mad after her beauty and popular for all those women eaters whose objective is nothing but to serve and enjoy the beauty of women. Very soon, the popularity of Sundara reaches to climax with every person in an around Harihareshwara begins his day uttering the name of Sundara. Overnight Sundara attains all that she wants. Her lovers make a splendid Haveli for Sundara which becomes popular as 'Sundara's Haveli' at the outskirt of the town. Being a whore, she prefers to keep herself away from the festivals celebrated in the town.

There is festive atmosphere everywhere in Hariharshwara. People are preparing for Ganpati

Visarjan Procession. The devotees are decorating the vehicles with marigold garlands. The technicians are checking the sound system which will be used during the procession. On the trial tune of the musical systems, the children are seen taking some dance steps. The procession begins and it goes through the various lanes of Harihareshwara. It is just behind the haveli of Sundara, there is a huge and historical water lake where the people of Harihareshwara do the visarjan of the idols of their lord Ganesha. When the procession comes and takes a pause at Sundara's haveli, Sundara comes out and stands in the gallery of haveli and takes a glimpse of the procession and darshan of Lord Ganesha. It seems that the procession is dying to have the rare glimpses of Sundara's beauty. After this brief pause, the procession reaches to its destination.

It is at the early hours of the dawn of the next day, the entire Harihareshwara gets shaken with the severe vibrations of earthquake which continue for ten minutes. In a brief period of ten minutes, the severe earthquake demolishes the entire town of Harihareshwara which took years to make its existence. Dawn disappears to let the Sun throw the light on the scene of demolition. The sunlight presents such scenes of destruction that makes one close his eyes as eyes would never like to see such a heart breaking scene of destruction. When splendid bungalows and houses are dancing on the instruction of the earthquake and falling one after the other, Sundara hurriedly comes out of her haveli stands still and sees with her open eyes the destruction of the entire town of Harihareshwara and her own haveli too is not an exception to this demolition. To add to this disaster, there comes the rain which further aggravates the situation. Dilapidated structures and dead bodies get mingled with mud and become difficult to identify which is mud and which are dead bodies. Sundara's eyes catch nothing but the mud of dead bodies of the people everywhere. Loss of lives is so colossal that it becomes question who would mourn on whose death as a few people are left to shade tears on the death of their kinsmen.

On hearing the crying sound of the babies, Sundara runs in the direction of crying sound saves lives as much as possible. Some old men, women, widows and a few young men who are saved in this natural calamity, come to strengthen her hands without bothering of her status. The news of this earthquake spreads like a wild fire throughout the state. Soon demolished Harihareswhara becomes a place of fair. People gather like ants. Sundara gets happy with this crowd but soon she gets disappointed to see that the people are not there to shade tears but to grab property of the dead one. She gets shocked when she sees that the people are busy in discovering the bodies from the mud and grabbing and snatching the gold ornaments of the dead bodies lying in the mud. She feels that Harihareshwara is being twice looted. Despite this she continues her rescue work and saves lives as much as possible. In the initial days after the earthquake, the people of all cadres, government officials, M.L.A. M.Ps., Ministers at the state and a few from the Center visit the earthquake affected Harihareshwara to complete the formality.

The countries all over the world send their help to the earthquake affected Harihareshwara. After a few days of photo session work and shading crocodile tears, all take the leave of Harihareshwara leaving its people die in the miserable conditions. A lot of financial help comes from the countries all over world and from the central government too. But it gets finished till it reaches to Hariharshwara. The almost dead Harihareshwara keeps it's eyes on the way which would bring savior but its hope turns to be hopeless. Disposal of dead bodies being mixed with mud takes a lot of time which causes epidemics and creates health hazards to the survived.

Sundara realizes her responsibility to revive the dead Harihareshwara. A period of month passes after the first photo session formality, none of the government officials or ministers or the media come back to the town to take a note of destruction and living lives dying for help. For years, Harihareshwara survives without hospitals, schools, banks, cradle houses, libraries and without electricity which darkens the darkness of the evening. Media too have no time to pay heed to the state of affairs in Harihareshwara as it is busy in showing T.R.P. earning news. For months Harihareshwara leads an ignored life.

Sundara does not afford to wait any more for the coming of the savior. She herself becomes the savior of the town and is fully aware of the fact that at any cost, she has to revive her town. She decides to destroy herself to create her town. Construction through destruction becomes the principle of her life on which she leads her future journey. Sundara determines to take absolute advantage of her body for the betterment of her town. She goes to the district collector to bring help for her town. At this time the District Collector is engaged in a meeting with his subordinates. Sundara comes and talks with the peon sitting on a stool. The peon begins to stare and capture as much beauty of Sundara as he can in his eyes. The peon tells her that 'Saheb' is busy in the meeting till then you can sit here. While sitting on the bench outside the Collector's cabin, she notices that the peon is engrossed and ceaselessly staring at her. The meeting ends and the people go out. The peon goes in and conveys the message that a beautiful woman has been waiting for long time to see him. His 'Saheb' asks him to send the woman in. Sundara comes in and introduces herself, "I am Sundara, the whore of Harihareshwara." He gets dumbfounded to see a woman with a mesmerizing beauty standing in front of him. The Distict Collector has heard enough stories of the beauty of Sundara but he never had the opportunity to see her. When he sees the actual Sundara is standing in his office and begging for help, her beauty is such that it makes him mad and his eyes grow lusty and hungry for her beauty. He begins his chat with Sundara in his pinky Hindi.

"Tau aap hai Sundara! Bilkul Nam ki tarah hai aap. Aao Sundaraji! Kaise Anna Hua" without giving her chance to speak, he continues his talk. "Aapke aur aapki khubsurtike bare mey maine bahot suna or padha bhi hai. Aaj mauka mila aapko dekhneka, Sundaraji." Sundara without waiting for his permission to sit, she occupies the chair and answers to lusty questions. "Bahot Din ho gaye, Kohibhi government ka admi Harihareshwar mey aaya nahi. Log madat ki rah me hei. Aap kuch karo Sir." The district Collector feels proud and braggartly says, "Aap ko na kahena hamare bas mei nahin hai. App hame khush karo and ham aapko..... Ho sake to aaj Ghar pe khana Khane ko aajao. Sundara spends that night with the District Collector. After initial talk........ritual is performed.

Thus Sundara goes on knocking at the doors of M.L.A., M.Ps, Ministers and other official in everyone she meets the lusty eyes of the district collector who enjoys the feast of her beauty.

Sundara's magic shows its miracles. In a few days, the never ending help comes in Harihareshwara. At the instruction of the seniors, the government officials rush towards Harihareshwara. The work of renovation and rehabilitation takes acceleration. With disappearing time, the old Harihareshwara too disappears from the canvas of the present bidding farewell to its lovers. Harihareshwara emerges as an ultra modern city with all facilities. People become oblivion to the disappeared Harihareshwar but form a great sense of respect and reverence for a woman who becomes a legend of sacrifice for the people of Harihareshwara and the entire state. Every one fondly calls her 'Amma' a savior of Harihareshawara. This is the new incarnation of Sundara. She no longer remains 'Sundara the Prostitute' but a spiritual personality who is loved, respected, honoured and taken care of by all people. Her celebrity crosses the frontiers of the nations. Devotees and her lovers from all over the world visit her ashram and gets blessings of SundaraAmma. Considering her sacrifice for the betterment of the society, not only many countries but also the central government of India and of course the state too gets eager to confer upon her the most covetous honors on. Her Haveli is transformed into an ashrama which is always crowded with her devotees and admirers. Disappearing years steal not only the dimple from the beautiful cheeks of

'Sundara Amma' but also the disgrace which corrodes her inwardly. She grows sufficiently old always resting on the bed as she suffers from a severe and uncured disease. Treatment is on but the body has become too weak to respond to the power of medicines. All efforts are stopped to rejuvenate the dilapidated body of 'Sundara Amma'.

Ceaseless depletion of the body makes 'Sundara Amma' almost dead. It is on one evening, the setting Sun calls the soul of 'Sundara Amma' to accompany him to a never ending journey of life. The soul of 'Amma' responds and thus 'Sundara Amma' pays the debt of nature leaving behind her a never ending fountain of inspiration for sacrifice and adherence to the society. The news of 'Sundara Amma' death spreads like a wild fire. People like ants start hurrying towards the ashrama where dead body of 'Sundara Amma' is kept for last darshan. The crowd enhances leaves no ant like space for stepping on the ground. For the first time in the history of Harihareshwara, the town has experienced and seen such a crowd of people, the edge of which becomes difficult to be fixed. The funeral procession begins and goes through every lane of Harihareshwara. Her lovers and devotees occupy whichever the place and space they get to take the last darshan of their 'Goddess'. The rain begins and it seems to all that the Nature is too shading tears on death of her darling soul. Harihareshwara gets drowned in the flood of tears. The sacrifice of Sundara not only immortalizes her but Harihareshwara as well.

Funeral procession continues for hours. On the last edge of the crowd, the two old gentle men who are the eye witness of Sundara's journey and transformation from a whore to a goddess are seen engaged in a serious conversation with tearful eyes. One says:

"Choice of making of a person is not in one's hands, it is destined. Despite of his strong will, one has to go with the option of life which one has never desired. Destiny traps persons in such net of miserable and helpless circumstances that they have to accept the things as they come in their lives does not matter whether they were their choices or not. A person born and brought up in any kind of family or any kind of the class or strata of the society never wants to go on such a track where he or she would be most undesirable, disgraced and unacceptable figure for the society. A gentle-man never wants to be a criminal of any sort but he is made. A decent woman does not matter, born or brought up in rich or a poor class never wants that the society should call her as whore or a prostitute which is nothing but a curse to entire woman's community. But they are made so not by themselves but by the society which itself gives birth to this darker and brighter side of its reflection. Sometimes it happens that a person preferably a decent woman who becomes the victim of treacheries at the hand of the destiny and unwillingly accepts the disgrace of being a prostitute. It should be remembered that it is power and miracle of destiny which makes a bad person good and vice versa. If the destiny wants it can make a beggar rich overnight and a millionaire a beggar dying for a penny. If the destiny wants it can make a decent woman as a whore or prostitute and vice versa. This is nothing but an endless unpitying but pleasant game of the destiny on which the entire world runs laughing and drowning into the never ending flood of tears. It is really a great pastime for the destiny of which we are all willingly or unwillingly inseparable parts. The happening of the things in the lives of the person are controlled by the destiny either by herself or through its agents such as the society which is responsible for making itself good or bad."

Other gentleman agrees with his friend and exclaims, "A woman is not a born prostitute but she is made!"

Divided Love

There is a two storied building in one of the lanes of Ulhas Nagar. The building has pious look and moral existence and is looked at with a sense of respect and pride by all those who reside around it. The building is named as Nishigandh and really there is a tree of Nishigandh which keeps the surrounding always fresh and fragrant. Anyone who passes by that building deliberately takes a pause to please his senses with the sweet smell of this philanthropic tree. On entering the hall of the building, the eyes catch a sufficiently big photo frame of Dr. Sarvapalli Radha Krishnan displayed on the wall which further enhances the holiness of the building. One more thing which glorifies this smelling building is the presence of a socially dedicated and illustrious couple of Mr. Ramakant Thakur and Mrs. Bharati Thakur both serve as the teachers in local secondary school. They have a son to whom they lovingly call Nayandeep. The name of the son indicates the importance of the presence of this son in their life. They love and care him as their soul. Their existence is nothing without this boy. They are very much focused and obsessed with this boy as they look at him as their future support and security and a mechanism of their wish fulfillment. The couple has been very active in all the fields. In addition to their academic responsibilities, the couple associates themselves with various social activities which give them a good name, fame and recognition. They live less for themselves and more for the society. Such is the commitment of the family to the society that they forget that they also have their own life priorities. Considering their academic accomplishments and their commitments to the society, the state government honors them as the ideal teachers which expand the roots of their fame and recognition. Everyone in Ulhas Nagar holds a great respect for this couple. Their house is always noisy with continuous presence of their acquaintances. Thus they grow very meticulous about their status in the society. With passing time their fame increases like that of a celebrity and they become status conscious and never do such thing which would harm it and never let anyone to do it.

As being the teachers and fully engaged in their activities, they hardly find time to spend with their son. So they have managed a girl who looks after Nayandeep in their absence. Thus the little boy is deprived of motherly and fatherly affection. Whole day he sits at the window waiting for his parents and bearing and enjoying confinement imposed by his parents due to their engagements. When his boredom touches the sky and solitariness eats him, he irritatingly asks the girl caretaker, "Where are my Mummy and Pappa? When will be they back? I am fed up with this loneliness. It seems to me that they love their earnings more than me. I am growing worthless. There perennial absence makes me feel to be an orphan." The caretaker tries to pacify him saying, "Calm down dear. They will be back soon. Don't think otherwise. I think your mind thinks too much." In waiting for his parents, he does not understand when the day breathed the last. They rarely get the chance to have a talk with him as they go early on their mission when he is in bed and return home late when they find him again to be in bed. Whenever the couple returns home early he catches and holds them so tightly as if he is meeting them after a long interval and gives an outlet to his inner feelings. "Don't leave me alone, Mamma. I am scared of the isolation which accompanies me whole day. Either be with me or take me with you. I miss you both". Mrs. Bharti Thakur tries to calm him down. "Don't cry my dear. We too don't want to leave you at home but we are helpless. Being away from you is the demand of the time. But don't worry everything will be alright soon." This thought of the mother convinces this little innocent boy and lives on the hope that soon his loneliness will come to an end and he will be free from this confinement. Thus he continues his life for some more days on this hope. He rarely gets the chance to have a talk with them and when they get time and want to talk with him, the sleep overpowers his long waiting and unfulfilled will. Nayandeep's stomach is always full with food but his hunger for motherly affection remains unfulfilled.

One day the parents of Nayandeep decide to send him to a school. They get him admitted in the first standard in a local school which is at a walking distance from their bungalow. But they don't send him alone. They manage an auto-rickshaw which takes him to school and brings back home. Thus his growing age and schooling demand breaks his confinement and brings him into the main stream of life. Seeing smiling, rejuvenating and pretty faces of other children, his passion for life gets strengthened and rejuvenated. In a short period of time he makes a good friend circle who becomes a cause of rare smile on his face. When he returns home, he eagerly waits for the coming of the tomorrow so that he can be in the school and with his friends chatting and doing fun tirelessly. Sunday is the favorite day for him as he gets the company of his parents. Whole day goes in doing masti and mischief. At evening hours he is taken to the nearby garden where he gets the chance to be with other children like him. Being with the new faces and playing new games become a great source of recreation for him. Parents also feel sad at heart as their social commitments keep them away from their loving son but they know that they are helpless but whenever they are free, they be with him and give him all that he wants. Their house is well decorated with presence of a lot of colorful toys which show their liberality of spending money on the pleasure and recreation of their son. After their professional and social commitments, Nayandeep is their prime concern and the topmost priority. Nayandeep is also happy with his position in the family and he lives in the hope that it will be maintained throughout life.

The Thakurs take the second chance. Seeing the growing stomach of his mother Nayadeep innocently asks her mother. "Are you alright? Is anything wrong with you?" Smiling at him and his concerned face, Mrs. Bharati questions him. "What makes you concerned, my dear?" Nothing is wrong with me. I am perfectly fine." Continuing his series of questions Nayandeep expresses the cause of his concern. "You say that nothing is wrong with you but see your stomach is overgrowing which makes me feel that you are sick and you are hiding it out from me." She takes him close and then lifts him and kisses him number of times and tells him the reason. "My darling, there is nothing to worry. A new baby is going to come in our house to accompany and play whole day with you." Raising his eyebrows with surprise, he questions further, "New baby! How pleasant! When will it come?" Hurriedly she shuts his mouth so that he could not question further. "He will come very soon, my dear. OK stop questioning and go to play. I have a lot of things to do."

A few days later, a new baby boy comes in their house. Nayandeep is very happy as he thinks that the baby will be his companion to play when the parents will be away from him. He goes to school in a very cheerful mood and tells all his friends that he has got a brother. The newly born baby is named Amardeep. Once Amardeep is lying on the cot, Nayandeep goes to love and care him. He tightly holds his cotton like cheeks in his hands which makes the baby cry. Hearing the cry of Amardeep mother comes hurriedly and tells him that he should not do like this because the baby is delicate and it can hurt him. He gets shocked with the way his mother removed his hand. It makes him question to himself "Am I a foe to hurt him?" The next time it happens that Nayandeep is throwing a ball against the wall and enjoys catching it. Accidently, the ball slipped out of his hand dashed against playing Amardeep on the cot. Anticipating that Nayandeep might have done wrong her darling baby, mother comes there slaps and pushes him down which hurts him. He gets bewildered and terrified by the sudden change in treatment of his mother. He realizes that his position is not safe as his mother has become absolutely Amardeep centered. Gradully, he feels that he has been thrown out of the circle as most of the time mother seems to be engaged with Amardeep and pays no heed to the needs of him. He thinks that his mother has got a substitute for him and he is not needed now. A question of self-existence starts troubling him.

Previously when Amardeep was not there, the mother used to ask the nurse whether Nayandeep took his food on time or not. Whenever she was at home, she used to run after Nayandeep and forcefully put the food in his mouth. But now such thing does not happen. He thinks that his Mummy has become so engaged in Amardeep that she forgets to make it sure whether Nayandeep has eaten or not. His little mind thinks that his mother has grown very much conscious and serious about the feeding of her younger son. Feeling of being marginalized gets further aggravated when he observes that not only mother but his father also has changed a lot in his treatment. Once, the family goes to a moll to shop. Seeing a beautiful horse which allures him, he wants his father to give him the horse. Hearing this father gets irritated and dishearten him saying, "Nayandeep you are not a little baby to play with toys. Instead of playing you need to concentrate on the study which will make you big enough to support us when we will be old." Suddenly Amardeep starts crying for a toy, Mr. Thakur paying an instant heed at the crying Amardeep buys that toy. This differentiating treatment hurts him. He thinks that when I demanded he said no and paid no heed to my demand. When Amardeep demanded, he gave him instantly. This difference in treatment of his father who once loved him and fulfilled all his demands hurts him. He doubts that the love of his parents is fake one and selfish as they expect support from him in their old age.

He gradually realizes that he has lost that position which once he felt proud of. Gradually the parents become Amardeep centered rarely paying heed to the needs of Nayandeep which makes him think that he is thrown out of that circle of affection and care where he once used to be. It seems to him that he is an excluded member whose presence in the family matters but very little. The change occurred in his once loving parents hurt him a lot and his stream of thinking takes a different turn. He grows indifferent towards the parents who for him are selfish and careless. He gets affected by the inferiority complex and develops a feeling that he is a solitary creature. Even in the school, all ask him about his brother Amardeep which makes him think a lot about changing preference of his parents and friends as well. So all these things make him think that he has grown worthless and has no existence of his own.

He grows in years entering a new standard but his academic results do not satisfy his parents. The more the parents expect from him, the more he spoils their hopes. When the mother is at home, she makes bombardment of questions regarding the completion of study but never takes him close and asks him what does he want? What hurts him is that she is conscious of what she wants from him but why she is ignorant of what he expects from her. He thinks that his parents always give the first priority to their social commitments and their commitments to their younger son. He asks himself why they are forgetful about their duties towards him. Now he reaches in his tenth. The parents expect that he would do something worth admiring in his examination. They always ask him about his study and they find that he is avoiding. They scold him but never try to make analysis of his indifference. The chaos of priority causes a chaos in his mind which affects him. He overcomes the exam but his result does not satisfy the ambitious expectation of his parents. He lowers down in their esteem as he breaks their dreams. They grow harsh in their treatment. When the father finds that Nayadeep is neglecting his studies he says in annoying tone, "you are a useless creature. We always look at you as our support in our old age but it seems to us that we have to be your support. Not for us, for your bread sake do something, you stupid fellow." This selfish assertion of the parents hurts him and thinks him that they feed and educate him because they want the returns of it.

Nayandeep becomes the student of science. Any how he completes his first year and now he is in twelfth, the most important year which decides the future course of Nayandeep and also the most expecting year for his parents. The discriminating conditions at home provoke him to go astray. Soon, he joins a company of vagabonds in the college which hampers his academics. Most of the times he bunks the lectures and seen on the playground. Once he gets involved in the quarrel which makes the college send a letter to the parents. When the parents come to know about the progress graph of their son, they visit the college without informing Nayandeep. But they get shocked to see that Nayandeep is not there. The Principal of the institute speaks in an irritating tone about Nayandeep. He says that considering their status, they have not taken any stern action against him. But the water is flowing overhead and they cannot entertain anymore the waywardness of their son. He complains that his presence in the college is detrimental to the academic conditions and gives them the warning if their son does not amend, the college management will take a stern action against him. Parents go home and wait for Nayandeep. He comes home late in the evening. Mr. Ramakant Thakur asks him somewhat angrily, "Nayandeep where have you been whole day?" Anticipating that father would be ignorant of his absence at the college says, "I was in the college attending lectures and practicals." Without questing further, father starts beating him with a stick and beats him black and blue with an improving thought it would amend his conduct. But impact of this beating does not last for a long and he returns on his usual track. Once, one of the boys from his group tries to molest a girl. When it happens Nayandeep is there supporting his friend. The college and the parents of the girl take the matter to the Police station. The police arrest Nayandeep and the boy on the accusation of molesting the girl. When the Thakurs reach the police station they feel guilty as throughout their lives, they have never climbed the step of it and what annoys them is that it is because of their spoiled son they have to do it. Using their influence, they get him free.

He is brought home. Mr. Ramakant a man who leads for his repute in the society, shuts the door so that the world outside should not laugh any further at them. But the news gets leaked and the colony comes to know about the misdeed of their son. The Thakurs decide that they would not let their son spoil their repute anymore. For the sake of their status which they have earned sacrificing the valuable years of the lives, they decide to sacrifice their son. They tie his hands legs and confine him in a store room for many years. When the neighbors and the acquaintances in the colony ask the Thakurs about the whereabouts of their elder son, they silence their questioning mouth by posing an excuse that he has been sent to their relatives in Dadar for his further studies. Early in the morning and when they return from the schools in the evening, they visit the dark room opens the rope tied to Nayandeep's hands and legs so that he can feed himself. The dark life has an adverse impact on the psyche of Nayandeep. He becomes somewhat aggressive and eccentric.

Once it happens that Mr. Ramakant Thakur goes out of station on an important mission. In his absence Mrs. Thakur takes the responsibility to feed the confined son. One evening when she opens the door, Nayandeep overpowers her and runs away and reaches to Pune. Mrs. Thakur wants to shout but she cannot do as it will inform the whole colony about their misdeeds. Late in the night when Mr. Ramakant Thakur returns home, Mrs. Thakur fearfully intimates him about the incident. He looks at her smiling says, "Thank God! You saved us from trouble." They decide to hide out the things from the world so they deliberately register no complaint in the local police station about sudden disappearance of their son. They are happy that their painful concern has ended and feel free to focus on their most promising son, Amardeep. He is good at studies. His studies reports please the parents. They provide him all that he wants with the expectation that he would make their future when they will be old. Amardeep knows how his parents have ill-treated his elder brother. But out of his love and affection and respects he feels for them, he silences his mouth on the matter. Amardeep being an obedient son and fully mature knows his responsibility. He studies hard and brings laurels to his family by passing every exam with scintillating success. He scores good in H.S.C and gets admitted in M.B.B. S. The parents are very happy with the way their darling son is climbing the ladder of success. With every successful steeping of their son, they feel more secured.

Meanwhile, Nayandeep works as a labor at various construction sites in Pune. During his life as a labor, Nayandeep acquires all the skills of constructions which make him stand high in the esteems of the renowned builders who always wish to have him on their construction sites. One of the builders considering his construction skills asks him to take the charge of his office and motivates him to continue his education. Nayandeep utilizing the support of his master completes his education in civil engineering through distance education and independently starts his business. Being in the field of construction for many years, he has established good contacts with the costumers. He starts getting contracts and soon he becomes one of the affluent builders in Pune region. He gets married with a girl who is also civil engineer who looks after his business.

Here in Ulhas Nagar, The Thakurs are happy as their son has taken the exam of final year of M.B.B.S. and eagerly waits for the day of his result. The day of result comes and happy and confident Amardeep gets up early in the morning gets fresh and takes darshan of Gods in frames and his parents before leaving the house to bring his result. He takes out his favorite bike and goes to the college. The result is declared late in the afternoon. Hungry and long awaiting Amardeep takes a breath of relief on receiving passing result. He hurriedly takes out his bike and drives home. When he is in the crowdy market, he receives a phone call of father. Handling his speedy bike with one hand and with the other he hastily takes out the ringing phone and very happily and proudly conveys the news of his success. While he is struggling to push in his cell phone in his tight trouser, suddenly an uncontrolled truck comes towards him. To save his bike from getting dashed, he speedily turns his bike and gets dashed against the compound wall by the side of the road. The crowd gathers and takes the unconscious Amardeep to hospital. The parents are informed about the accident. They reach to the hospital controlling their scared and dying breaths. The mishap is so horrible that Amardeep receives a severe injury to his brain which needs to be operated. Parents spend whatever they have on the life of their son. But the fortune does not smile on them. Doctors do all that is possible but they do no miracle and the dead body of Amardeep is handed over to his half dead parents.

The Thakurs undergo a great depression. They have everything but they have nothing. They have earned a lot in their lives but the question troubles them is to whom it should be given. They are the richest but none is poorest like them. A kind of hollow is created in their lives due to unexpected departure of their two sons. The room where they had locked their first son Nayandeep eats them and troubles them with its memories. They feel extremely sad at heart but what is the value of the tears which are delayed. Not only their house but the entire Ulhas Nagar becomes hot for them. The memories of their loving sons steal their lives. Nights become the days for them. When they look at the tree in the front yard of their bungalow, it seems to them the tree has stopped releasing smell as if it is unhappy at heart. Being troubled with bitter memories the Thakurs sell out their properties and go to Pune. There they associate themselves with an NGO which works for the betterment of the orphans. The Thakurs think that there is no other better way than this to take penance for what wrong they have done to their children. The NGO offers them a flat in its hostel and thus begin their routine trying and pretending to forget the memories of their sons.

One day after their shopping they are taking dinner in a hotel. At a little distance from their table a young and charming well dressed person is chatting with his equally cultured person. Suddenly Mr. Ramakant Thakur identifies the person facing him to be his son Nayandeep. He loudly calls his name, the moment this voice falls on the ears of Nayandeep, he looks at the person calling within no time he identifies his father. Both meet and embrace each other. They take dinner together. During Dinner the parents narrate the story of their setbacks. Nayandeep also becomes emotional. But forgetting for a moment what happened to their second son Amardeep they become happy with the way their most unworthy son has become the worthiest. Considering the plight of the parents, Nayandeep requests them to come to his home and be there with him permanently. They reach home. They talk till late in the night but he finds that his father avoids meeting his eyes. Nayandeep introduces them to his wife. All become happy but in some deep corner of their hearts the Thakurs find themselves to be guilty. This guilty consciousness does not let them sleep there throughout the night. They grow uneasy and wait when the night ends. In the morning they come with their bags. Nayandeep feels strange and he asks, "Pappa why these bags for? You have just come to stay with us and where do you plan to go so early?" Mr. Ramakant Thakur tries to convince his son, "My dear, we are going back to the hostel as we cannot stay here for very long." Nayan tries to snatch away their bags but the Thakurs becomes too obstinate to go. Mr. Ramakant Thakur says to his son, "My dear, whenever I look at you, my mind takes me back to our past and reminds me all that harshness, cruelty and discrimination we had done to you. You may have forgotten but we can't. Our deeds won't let us lead calmly until we pay price for what we have done to you. Really, we made a colossal mistake. We differentiated and unequally treated you and your brother. We never thought that making difference would make us pay so heavily. Advising their son "Don't differentiate." They leave him with a sense of happiness and satisfaction that at least their one son is alive and doing well in his life. They reach to their hostel to lead for those who never have seen their parents.

A Flower of Wisdom

It is the late hour of the morning, stepping sound of a Professor vibrates the serene corridor of an educational institute located at secluded and forest like area of Sita Nagari, swiftly advancing and expanding city. The Professor has recently joined this institute and is not thoroughly acquainted with every nook and corner of the college edifice. During an hour of leisure, he takes a round to see the premise of the college. During his round he observes that his staff mates and the students are engrossed in enlightening stream of knowledge. When he reaches to the last class-room of the third floor somewhat isolated smells the happening of something undesirable. Protesting cry of a girl troubles the ears of the Professor. Anticipating the happening of something undesirable, hurriedly he opens the door slightly pushed from inside and finds a girl and boy students are engaged in ferocious contention. On probing, the girl tells that she has been brought forcefully here and the boy is trying to molest her. Professor loses his senses and scolds the boy very harshly. Not bearing this insult, the student suddenly enters the 'Macbethan World' and beats the teacher black and blue. On seeing the unexpected things happening, girl gets terrified and bewildered and starts running to the Principal's Cabin and narrates the whole incident happened. Principal and staff members rush towards the disputed classroom and find that teacher lying on the ground unable to get up as he can't bear severe punches and blows of the boy. Meanwhile the accused boy escapes from the spot. Professor is taken to Principal's cabin for relief.

The news of the beating the Professor spreads in every nook and corner of the college. The event becomes breaking news of almost all Media. Professor cannot tolerate this defame and stops going to the college. The event corrodes him inwardly and steals his confidence to face his students, his staff and of course the people around. One day at the midnight hour finding his wife and little son asleep, hangs him to the ceiling fan. The next day, once again Professor's suicide grabs the front page of almost all the newspapers.

Police investigation begins as the matter is highly sensitive. The accused boy is caught and presented before the court. Considering the sensitivity of the matter and to prevent the students from doing such reckless deeds, the court gives the accused boy a severe punishment of lifelong imprisonment. The accused is put behind the bar. The family of Professor cannot bear the unexpected blow of the destiny. Adversities start assaulting on the family of the Professor makes it as weaker as possible. Confused and sullen wife of the Professor toils and moils to find the ways of the survival of her little family. Anyhow she succeeds in getting a menial job which consolidates the family's hope to live.

Life begins its life in darkness of the cell and writes such philosophy of life which moves the human hearts. Breathing and snoring sound of a human body steals the tranquility of the cell. It is the breathing and snoring sound of the accused boy resting in the dark and dirty corner of the cell. The first rays of the Sun peep through the small window of the cell and fall on the faceless face of the accused boy. The name of the accused boy is disclosed from the police records and it is Raju. Professor's words make such an incurable wound to his ego that it does not make him feel to lament on what he has done. It seems that he is still lingering in the Macbethan world where foul is fair and fair is foul. It takes a lot of time to take him out of the influence of Macbethan world. Time just goes on turning the pages of months and years of yearly calendar of Raju's life. He grows in years and dark rooms and dark confinements of the cell plant roots of wisdom in him. Black hair on the top of Raju start turning white which symbolize and mark the blooming of a bud of maturity in him. The dark confinement of the jail and its boredom steal his anger and transforms him into a mild but barred gentleman.

The dark confinements teach him a lot. His boredom makes him restless. He struggles to do something which would kill this boredom and make his barred life somewhat ease and pleasant. One day while loitering in the confined premise of the jail, a plant of a newly bloomed red rose steals his attention. He goes to the plant and looks at its beauty and freshness. It seems to him that it is giving him a message to be happy in all the situations makes others happy. It seems to him that the red rose plant is telling him that it is also confined but not stopped living and ceaselessly spreading and giving happiness for others. As it does he too can. The beauty of the red rose beautifies his ugly mind. Raju slowly grows sensitive to the feelings. His mind suddenly turns to be poetic and thinks that life would be really worth living and worth enjoying if it ever be blessed with presence of such beautiful roses. His interest grows in that plant. After taking his meal, he returns to his nest in the dark and hopeless womb of the darkness in the cell.

One day a sound of sewing machine falls on his ears at the late hours of the evening which steals his sleep. He grows curious to know where it comes from and what it is about. When he peeps through the gap of iron bars of his cell he finds that a widow wearing a white sari is taking pains on the sewing machine. The sound of sewing machine continues to steal his attention till late in the night. Before going to bed with the end of sound of sewing machine he determines to know about the woman. During his initial years in the confinement of the jail, he establishes a good rapport with the Jailor who too is happy with improvement in the conduct of Raju. The next day he meets the Jailor and expresses his curiosity to know about the woman. Being friendly with Raju, he briefly narrates him what happened with the woman.

He tells him that the woman is imprisoned on account of murder charge. In a tone of worry and sympathy he tells him that the husband of the woman was a great drunkard. The irresponsible and drunkard father caused great suffering to her and her five years old son. Every day he used to come home and beat his wife (woman in the jail) and sometimes beat his little son which she could not tolerate. One day there was contention between husband and wife. Husband somewhat unconscious and influenced by the taste of wine tried to strike to his wife with an iron rod. During contention she too grew ferocious and unknowingly and being fed up with that routine trouble of her husband angrily held his hand in protest took out the iron rod and hit on his head in retort. Her husband died on the spot. She kept her little son with her neighbor as she had no blood relations. The jailor tells him that the woman does some sewing work to earn some money. Raju interferes in the middle when his curiosity is at its zenith and asks the jailor what does she do with the money? Jailor realizes that Raju has taken the story very seriously and without stretching his intensity he ends the record of woman's life saying that the woman sends her earned money to her son so that he can continue his studies.

The woman's story moves his heart. He thinks of his deed and its impact on the life of a fatherless family. Imagined suffering family of Professor brings tears in his eyes. The flint hearted Raju gets melted before the fire of suffering of Professor's family. A thought 'It is never too late to amend' strikes his Macbethan World. Raju's melted heart becomes mild and smooth and revives new Raju who determines to live for others and thinks that there is no other way to take penance than this. While taking morning walk in the surroundings of the jail, he happens to visit the rose plant. While looking at the enchanting beauty and realizing the philosophical purpose behind its presence, an idea clicks in his mind. Instantly, he reaches to the cabin of the Jailor and expresses his heartfelt desire to take penance for what he has done. He expresses his desire to undertake developing a nursery work in the jail. The Jailor gets impressed by the changed Raju and his strong will. The jailor assures him of all possible support and help on his side.

His pain and dreams become a great accomplishment. In this nursery he produces different varieties of roses which become the great demand of the outside market. Raju succeeds in attaining a good and sound source of income which he wishes to spend for the happiness of others. Suddenly, the gloomy picture of suffering wife or murdered Professor and his innocent and deprived son steals his mind. He goes to the Jailor and expresses his will to help the Professor's family. Jailor is very much moved by philanthropic change in Raju. Raju requests him that he wants to have the information about the family of Professor and if possible make available the bank account number of the family and requests him further not to disclose his name and tell the fake cause to the family that the government needs it to deposit some financial help for the sake of family. Being moved by noble desire of Raju, he responds positively. On the very next day the Jailor gives him the details of the family and its bank account number and does not forget to tell him the Professor's family still resides in Sita Nagari. Raju's nursery business flourishes very swiftly and gives Raju a good earning. After an interval of a month, he meets the jailor and renders him some amount and begs him to deposit it in the account of Professor's family. Jailor, out of affinity for Raju and being impressed by his philanthropic change, takes the trouble of periodically depositing Raju's earned money in the bank account of Professor's family.

Professor's family gets a great financial relief which they suppose it to be the blessing of the government.

It helps the wife of Professor to complete the study of her lonely son. She is lucky enough that she has a very obedient and academically sharp son who pleases the family with his academic accomplishments. Months and years pass and Mahesh becomes a doctor. One day he expresses his desire to his mother that he wants to start his own hospital. Mother responds positively and strengthens his wings of ambition. Her bank account has become very sound with ceaseless flow of money. She hands over some amount out of it to her loving son to build his own hospital. Her son's dream to have his own hospital comes true and with his outstanding service he emerges as a popular doctor in Sita Nagari. Every one fondly calls him Dr. Mahesh.

Meanwhile, Dr. Mahesh gets married and has two little kids. His wife is also a doctor and acts as helping hand to Mahesh. One day, when the family is enjoying meal together at night, Mahesh's mother speaks about the never ending flow of money deposited in her account. After hearing it Mahesh also gets shocked and surprised at never ending flow of money and its source. He doubts that what his mother says that it comes from Government. He is mature enough to understand that the government is not that much liberal to provide such never ending financial help. He makes up his mind to reach to the doubtful and somewhat mysterious derivation of the never ending flow of money. The next day, when he is in his leisure, he visits the bank and gets shocked to know that it is not the government but the Jailor who has been depositing the money in his mother's account. He smells the presence of some mysterious element in it. On the very next day, he visits the jail and finds that the jailor is enjoying his lunch.

He humbly waits till the jailor finishes his lunch. After a short interval of time he meets the jailor. The jailor uncovers the truth. Mahesh expresses his strong desire to see once upon time's Raju turned Raju Babu. The meeting puts his thinking hut on fire. He returns home. Mind is pregnant with the record of meeting. After his meal, he goes to his mother's bed room and narrates the whole mysterious record. On hearing it mother gets moved for time being forgetting what Raju has done to her husband. Mahesh begins the discussion with a little bit negative tone saying that it is somewhat difficult to pardon and accept a person who has wronged his family. Mother listens to him and presents her philosophically touched argument which brings the discussion to its positive end. Mother tells her son that there is no doubt that Raju has done a great injustice to the family but at the same time he too has suffered a lot for what he has done. He has taken enough penance and what he has done for her family is really moving and worth admiring. She records it without fail that it is just because of Raju, they could be what they are now. She philosophically projects her attitude that wisdom lies in forgetting what he had done with his father and further adds that wisdom demands to ever remember what he has done to her and her son. She continues her philosophical talk which makes him admit that there is no sense in digging out the bones of history but to construct the history with newer perspective. She means to say that it is better to forget the dark presence of the past of Raju and pardon him with his presence. In short, she teaches him the lesson of amnesty. They willingly decide to pardon the innocent crime of Raju and offer him a chance to lead a disgrace free life.

The next day when Mahesh visits the jail and gets informed that the government has decided to reduce the punishment years of Raju Babu on account of his good conduct and tomorrow he would be released from the jail he thinks that the time has offered him a unique opportunity to help the man who has made his life. The jailor informs the relatives about the release of Raju alias Raju Babu but nobody comes to receive him on the day of release. The jailor receives a written letter from the distant relatives of Rajubabu informing that they have no interest in Rajubabu and don't wish to have any kind of association with the person whose history is disgraced. After reading the letter of the relatives of Rajubabu, the Jailor feels hurt at heart and controlling himself he conveys the message to Rajubabu. Rajubabu does not get shocked by this anticipated response. Suddenly his eyes catch Mahesh approaching towards him. Before departing, Rajubabu affectionately and friendly shakes hands and embraces the jailor saying 'Thank you very much for your goodness, my dear Jailor."

Mahesh urges him to come and stay with him in his hospital. He offers him a flat in the hospital and begs to give him a chance to serve the man who made his life. Rajubabu heartily agrees and spends his remaining years serving patients in the hospital. Mahesh experiences, feels and enjoys the fatherly presence of Rajubbu. One day, Rajubabu receives a severe heart attack. Mahesh makes sincere efforts to save his Rajubabu but he fails. Perhaps destiny is happy with his penance and doesn't want that Rajubabu to suffer anymore. Mahesh and his family gets very much shocked and moved by the sudden departure of their support. Mahesh as a son completes and performs all the rituals of funeral. A huge sized and garlanded photo frame of Rajubabu is displayed in the hall of the hospital which ceaselessly inspires Mahesh to go on the path of goodness.

Success

'Success Is Counted Sweet By Those Who Never Succeed'. It is with this popular philosophical thought, it seems that life begins of a family headed by an unsuccessful writer, Mr. Prafulchandra living in an ancestral small sized house always in an ever repairing state in the town of Shivpuri. An entry into this long decaying house brings it to one's serious notice that the presence of potteries and utensils are almost eclipsed by the gigantic empire of books. There is a long row of systematically arranged shelves of books. It impresses anyone who peeps into this house that it is house cum library. It seems that air in this ever decaying literary house releases a never ending literary smell which pleases one's aesthetic senses. In one of the corners in the dark room where it seems that the entry of light of the Sun is deliberately prohibited, an ever ailing old woman is lying on the wooden cot counting her breaths and waiting for that moment when her heavy soul would get redemption from her weak and decayed body which is unable to bear the burden of soul. Ceaselessly decaying house along with ever ailing mother and arid aspirations of literary accomplishments of the so called writer Mr. Prafulchandra whose ink never writes a page of success contributes enormously to the troubles of the family. Their lives are nothing but a long waiting for that success and that forlorn hope that one day or the other literary talent of the writer, Prafulchandra, will change the fortune of ever decaying and destitute family. Disappointed and somewhat hopeless human voices are heard in the bedroom. They are of Mr. Prafulchandra and his ever supporting wife Bhagyamati and their two sons. The names of these two, husband and wife, seem to try to prove the futility of ironical sense of the question of a great writer, Shakespeare who says, "What's there in the name?"

By re-questioning, "What is not there in the name?" As if this great writer of the 16th century relates the name of the person to his destiny. The name of Bhagyamati stands for a woman of great fortune and the name of so called writer Mr. Parfulchandra means maintaining cheerfulness in all the circumstances.

Mr. Prafulchandra has been in the field of English literary writing since his bachelor life attempting his unsuccessful hand at the various literary forms such as novels, drama and poetry. He has been publishing his literary talents in a local news paper whose roots of existence never cross the frontiers of Shivpuri. In short, the fame of Mr. Prafulchandra as a writer remains confined and his literary creations remain unnoticed and unappreciated by the outside literary world. People of Shivpuri respect him but sometimes it seems that their respect is mocking respect. In his absence the people of Shivpuri makes fun of his literary talent and makes him a subject of criticism and mockery. As it is done in the absence of the so called writer who being credulous and innocent doesn't understand this derogatory and belittling view of the people in Shivpuri. He is very happy with his fame as a writer. When someone comes knocking at his door addressing him as 'Writer Saheb', his chaste gets pregnant with feeling of pride and happiness. To maintain his image as a writer and its popularity, the writer does all literary fetching and carrying for illiterate and semi- illiterate and sometimes literate people by helping them in their literary and non-literary works. The so called writer Mr. Prafulchandra has been publishing his literary talent in the local newspaper, the editor of which too unwillingly publishes his works as he has to fill the empty space in the news paper.

His published literary creations are great feast for both the men and wife they enjoy it till the coming of the next. With every publication, they get engrossed in building the castle in air that the one day or the other, the literary powers of the so called Writer Prafulchandra would give rise to such a 'classics' which would remove their inheritance of poverty by showering on them a ceaseless flow of affluence. It is this hope which becomes the reason of their happiness in all summers. Mr. Prafulchandra too is confident that one day or the other his literary fortune would smile upon him and fulfill his ever enshrined desire to be a writer of an international repute. Bhagyamati is an innocent wife and happy in lingering in the deceptive glamour of her husband's world of literary repute. She too is very happy with her husband's repute as writer. She admits with a feeling of pride that when the Writer's marriage proposal had brought to her and when she was told that the boy was a great writer, she accepted it with great happiness. When someone asks her about her husband addressing "Where is the writer sahib?" It makes her proud to be the wife of a writer who is very known figure of Shivpuri. Thus they go on spending their matrimonial life in the fake glamour of the world of self deception and suspension of disbelief.

The writer is called for various social gatherings and other less significant programs as a chief guest at various educational institutes and other organizations as there is no literary figure of his repute in Shivpuri. Sometimes he self willingly or sometimes on the invitation attends the poetry summit and other literary activities and reads out his literary creation without bothering what the audience thinks about his works. Ironical clapping response of the audience gives him happiness and with new vigor, he continues his literary presentation. In short he fails to understand that people have no genuine interest in his literary creations. Thus his credulous mind takes ironical applause of the audience to be a genuine praise of his literary and creative genius and lingers in this fake patting on his back of his audience throughout his life. The time goes on passing with aggravating economical conditions of the family. Neither the writer creates such a work of literary creation which can economically strengthen their lives nor does the editor of the local news paper make a proper economical valuation of his work. Thus financial source of the family grows weaker day by day. Considering the unlucky conditions of the husband, Bhagyamati tries to support financially the family by doing some sewing work. As a responsible wife and a great believer in the aspirations and ability of her husband, she keeps her family happy and keeps her husband's hope alive to be a writer of an international repute in all the times of ups and downs.

Once, Bhagyamati receives a notice calling her in the school. As Mr. Prafulchandra is out of station, she attends the call. The headmistress of the school tells her that the fee of both of their children is pending and if not paid, the school may take an action against them. On coming of the writer, she reveals the minutes of the meeting with the Headmistress. The writer raises his eyebrows in tension. He feels troubled with this. On the very next day, he goes to the editor to borrow some money promising that he would give the best possible literary creation. The editor ironically laughs at literary optimism of the writer and lends him the desired amount. Thus the Writer succeeds in overcoming this worry which marks the beginning of the other. Wailing sounds of his ever ailing mother intensify day by day enhancing the worries of the ever struggling Writer and his Wife. One day the illness of the mother becomes very serious and she is shifted to a nearby hospital. She undergoes a severe heart operation which contributes to the growing financial worries of the family. Ever ailing mother's operation demands such a huge amount which he has never seen in his life. His wife too has nothing sellable which can enable her to overcome this financial disaster of the time. Writer doesn't have that much credit in Shivpuri so that such a huge amount becomes accessible to him. For the first time, the Writer and his wife feel discouraged and sorry over their financial lot. They find that things are not manageable. As a responsible son he cannot let her loving mother die on the excuse of not having money. Finding no ways, they decide to take a mortgage loan against their ever decaying ancestral small sized house. They keep the documents of the house at the disposal of a rich person in the town and get the money. Operation is done successfully and mother comes home with ever ailing state as other diseases start corroding her body. A few days after the operation, the long awaiting soul of the mother takes the leave of her ever decaying body. Financially collapsed family cannot easily bear this blow of the destiny as it is taking the test of the never ending optimism of the Writer and his wife Bhagyamati. This is the dark period of the Writer's literary creation as no fruitful and economically benefitting work comes out of the Writer's creative brain. Wife's half of earning goes in paying the loan taken against the ever decaying ancestral house. The family decides to stop the schooling of their children as the family cannot afford its expenses. Her both sons help her in sewing business and soon start their tailoring shops which make them survive anyhow. Time goes ahead with that the family too suffering the blows of the destiny and with never extinguishing fire of optimism that their love and dedication for the field of literary creation would change their destiny.

One day the Writer unexpectedly falls ill. Slowly his illness takes a serious form continues for several months. Treatment goes but no medicine serves the purpose. Yet his optimism does not let him sit quietly. He picks up a pen and begins to write novel. Already troubled and worried wife hurriedly comes and tries to snatch away the pen and paper. For the first she blames her husband that his love for writing has murdered their dreams and aspirations spoiled the hope to live. Ignoring his wife's angry remark, he continues his work. His writing flowers with his flowering illness. One day he lovingly calls his wife and tells her that he has entitled his novel as "Success" and asks his wife to handover the manuscript of the work after its completion to the editor of the local newspaper. The next day the writer gets up early in the morning despite of his weakness he takes a round in his house looking at the long preserved books in the shelves as if he may not be there tomorrow to love and take care of them. Then he takes out all manuscripts of his literary creations from his wooden cupboard looks at them, removing the dust gives a last dying smile to them as if he is bidding farewell to them and puts them back in the cupboard. It is at the time when the slowly dying Sun reaches at the mid of the dismayed sky, he begins his writing. Hurriedly he finishes one page after the other as if he has smelt his approaching end of his life. It is at the Sunset, the Writer with greater haste completes the last page and puts a double full stop looking at the disappearing and reducing full stop like Sun on Horizon. A few days after writer's death, broken wife, Bhagyamati goes to the editor to handover the manuscript of the writer's last work. As a tribute to the writer and his past association, he publishes his novel in sections in his newspaper. Unfortunately it fails to arrest the attention of the literary world.

One day a worldly known Literary Critic comes to attend a Social Gathering of an educational institute in Shivpuri. Before going to the function, he is offered paper covered refreshment. While having his refreshment, suddenly a small word written in block letters SUCCESS catches his attention. He goes through it and gets overwhelmed by its content. He asks the organizer to collect the information about the paper which published it and expresses his desire to see the editor after finishing the function. One of the regular readers of the News paper 'Jagruti' identifies it and arranges the meeting. The Critic takes the manuscript of the Writer's novel *Success* and sends it to the world's the best publisher. The novel gets published and breaks the records of popularity showering ample affluence on the writer's family. The novel is translated in several languages all over world capturing the world's best prizes and honors. The writer's wife gets overwhelmed by the unprecedented success of his dear departed husband's book 'SUCCESS'. Affluence comes and all worries get vanished. The first thing she does is that she goes to rich man pays his debts with interest and gets back the property papers of her ever decaying ancestral house. She rebuilds it and makes it huge and splendid spending a lot and name it as 'The Writer's Cottage'.

As a tribute to her dear departed husband and to keep his memory alive, she starts a publishing house named Writer's Publishing House to give justice to many unnoticed and destitute literary genius whose creative talent does not reach to the frontiers of World literature. In too little time, the publishing house becomes the talk of the town receives ample literary creations of the literary figures in and around Shivpuri. An editing board is appointed to check the quality and standard of the literary works of the lovers of creative writing. The amateur writers' literary works wanting of quality are humbly suggested to make modifications and resubmit. Thus enough care is taken to see that the hopeful and enthusiastic emerging writers should not be disheartened. In the course of the time the Writer's publishing house creates ample classics and gives wonderful literary genius and creative writers who enrich the field of World Literature. Not only the nation but also the literary world beyond nation's boundary takes a serious note of it. The lovers of literature feel that once again the dark period of literature has gone paving the way for Renaissance of literature. Seeing the flourishing publishing house, Bhagyamati, innocently mutters, "How nice it would have been if the Writer had been alive to see this."

Essence of Life

There is hustle and bustle everywhere in the dining room and kitchen of a huge and enchanting bungalow located in the posh and high class society of Himayatnagar. The bungalow is named as Mr. Rajnandan's Cottage. Women's hasty and hurried voices are heard in the interiors of the cottage, some members of the family are seen hurriedly finishing their breakfast and leaving the splendid house for their daily routine. Some members are sitting at the dining table and eagerly waiting for their breakfast to be served. One of the elderly persons sitting at the dining table is Mr. Rajnandan, one of the most successful businessmen in the world of Jewlery. The fame of this successful business has spread all over the state. The existence of his business is seen in almost all the metropolitan cities of the state in the form of franchises of jewelry business. Rajnandan is of course a successful businessman but not like real successful businessmen who make the world of their business out of ash. Rajnandan is such a person who was born with silver spoon in his mouth. He is successful in the sense that he enhances and expands the inherited business of Jewlery from his father who too was a well known name of his time in jewelry business of Himayatnagar. The commendable business of Mr. Rajnandan is that he gives a state level recognition to his inherited business.

The interiors of the bungalow are really marvelous and heart stealing. It is skillfully and beautifully festooned with the world's outstanding artifacts. Every artifact garnishing bungalow symbolizes the affluence of Rajnandan. Every tour overseas adds to the beautifying artifacts of this bungalow. Everything whether it may be a sofa or dining tables, curtains, statues, furniture and other interior elements reflect the aesthetic sense and love for thing of luxury and of beauty of Mr. Rajnandan. It is seen and observed that in most of the bungalows in high class society, special portion is reserved for the pious existence of the library. Sometimes it is done to pretend to be cultured, aristocratic and scholarly family. One thing which is strikingly observed about Rajnandan's house is the absence of the library. One may find a lot of artifacts which release the smell of the riches of Rajnandan but no book lying here and there. It enhances the curiosity why is it so?

The answer of this is really shocking. Mr. Rajnandan is such a man who never loved books in his life. He spends thousands on the things of beauty and physical comfort but thinks hundred times to spend a single rupee on a book which beautifies one's intellect. Mr. Rajnandan opines that spending money on books is wastage of money. Today's read book is forgotten tomorrow and what gathers on it is a heap of detrimental dust. For him reading is worthless activity and idles away one's time. If the time wasted in reading, the baffling of the so called philosophical writers, is spent on business skills, he says with a great emphasis that the country would regain its status of the most affluent country in the world and once again the golden smoke would be released from the each and every nook and corner of the country that would shine the world. He blames that the poverty is the gift of that so called intellectuals who bury them in the books wasting time in the library and just building castles in the air with imagination and doing nothing in reality. He hates all the intellectuals and their intellectual society engrossed in playing the game of emotions and befooling the world. He asserts that it is just because of the successful businessmen like him; the nation is sound in affluence otherwise these intellectuals (book worms), so called emotional fools, doing nothing would have eventually bankrupt the nation. He says that these intellectuals resemble to those speaking parrots who speak but does nothing.

Mr. Rajnandan is a son born with silver spoon in his mouth. Being born and brought up in a business family had natural apathy for education. The family believed that education makes man emotionally rich and practically tame. The family was fully aware that their business is nothing but an output of their practical potential. Yet the father of Mr. Rajnandan had admitted him in the school. Mr. Rajandan joined the school but did not amalgamate himself with academic conditions in the school. He found the books of Mathematics and Social Sciences to be incomprehensible. Being unable to read and understand the incomprehensible and dead concepts in the study books, he lost his animation in academics and told his father that he would cease going to school from tomorrow. Father too did not force him as he knew that the blood of a businessman flows in his body which would not survive with the oxygen of books. A failure in academics aroused an apathetic feeling in him for books. Thus he never touched a book thereafter and fully dedicated to his father's business. At an early age of his life he started taking interest in his father's jewelry shop and within a short span of time; with his business skills he took his father's jewelry business to an unexpected height of success.

Rajnandan gets married and has two little sweet and handsome sons. Against his desire his sons are admitted in the school. He does so to respect his wife's emotions. Years chase each other; his sons grow in years passing one examination after the other. Once, his elder son, Rajdeep, requests his mother for new books. She takes him to his father. On hearing the demand, he scolds both saying that he cannot afford to spend money on books and orders his wife either to borrow books from the neighbors or buy the second hand books which would charge him less. He gets ready to spend money on second hand books to please his wife. Realizing her husband's opposition she goes to neighbor to lend books. The housewife of the neighbor feeling proud hurts the wife of Rajnandan saying, "you so called rich people can afford to spend a lot on the beautifying artifacts but feel troubled to spend pennies on books. Then what is the use of affluence which makes you beg to us?" The words of the neighboring housewife wound her ego so much and she determines that she would never beg to anyone. Realizing that money unnecessarily wasted on the education of his sons would not benefit his business, he decides to cease the education of his sons. Mother too feels helpless before an obstinate father who hates books. Every day Rajnandan takes his sons Rajveer and Rajdeep to his jewelry shop so that they can acquire business skills in their early age of their lives.

A year gets engulfed into the past with the birth of the next. Mr. Rajnandan moves the earth and the heaven to expand his business to its zenith. His sons too grow and with equal passion, support and strengthen his father's hand in business. Mr. Rajnandan always takes care that his family should enjoy every thing of beauty and comfort. He purchases most costly cars for his family. He takes care everything should be costly and beautiful. In this way he tries to keep his family happy with all luxuries of the world. Time grows older and with that young Mr. Rajnandan too. Gradually, he withdraws himself from the business handing over its responsibility to his mature and able sons. He showers his affluence on all the things of luxuries but the thought of buying worth reading books never touches him. It is his conviction that real pleasure or essence of life lies in the things of beauty and luxuries and not in the gathered heap of dust on the books and dusty pages of the books.

He spends a lot on all these beautifying objects and comfort and to add to this he takes his entire family on foreign tours. He looks it as a source of comfort and sign of being rich. He enjoys every possible pleasure in the world yet in the deep corner of his mind, he feels that real pleasure is yet to be felt and enjoyed.

The changing times steal his youth and his artificial pleasure which he takes in his riches. Gradually his sons start taking possession of the things which he has purchased with his pain. His motorcars are used by his sons; the key of his treasury goes at the disposal of his sons. He feels very disappointed to see the things which he took pride in and claimed to be his own are slipping out of his hand. One day he falls ill, he stares at the costly artifacts in his bedroom. He feels that the time has stolen their beauty and they have sufficiently become pale, unpleasant and uninspiring. Having watched them regularly; he loses his pleasure in them. He gets fed up with this monotonous beauty. His mind aspires and desires for eternal beauty and he comes to the conclusion that it is in vain to find it in the comforts and luxuries of the costly and antique artifacts which reflects his affluence. His mind is at fire to find the eternal pleasure. One day when he is having chat with his wife, he tells her that he has earned a lot and he is proud of it. After hearing this self-boosting assertion of her husband, she ironically nods and says "What is the use of the affluence which deprives her sons from their education which teaches them to lead a balanced life. My sons have become extreme materialists playing with the emotions of people. For me they are murderers of people's emotions. They exist at the cost of death of others. This is a success but a fake one. It gives me pleasure but feels it to be unpleasant."

He sinks himself in despair after knowing how low he stands in his wife's esteem. He thinks that he has earned a lot but he has lost more than what he has earned in his life. His feel of frustration is at apex. Once, a distant kinsman comes to enquire his health. While departing, he unknowingly forgets a book at the bed of Mr. Rajnandan. Initially he unnotices it deliberately and keeps it untouched as his inherent hatred for books tries to block the outlay of his search for real pleasure. But after some time, he undesirably picks it up, stares at the black and white world in it and ceases his staring at it with the last full stop in the book. After reading the book, he feels rejuvenated. He gets up from his bed, packs his bag and takes some money from his own source. He tells his wife and family that he is going on some mission and will take a long time to return. He leaves his family and affluence back, he reaches to a new city where he joins Vrudha Ashram named Anand Ashram. He spends hours in chatting and playing different games of amusement with old and senior citizens un-entertained and unnoticed by their blood relations. His obsession for eternal pleasure or real pleasure becomes his passion now. He joins a nearby library and he spends hours in reading spiritual and religious books. The money which he has brought with him uses it for buying new books and rare books which are not available in the library. His reading makes him so happy and gives him the peace of mind which he looks for. One day, when the sun is going to his bed, he takes a pen looking at vanishing beauty of the sun and starts writing. It proves to be an unpredictable and impossible thing that his pen writes such a book of wisdom which steals the intellect of the world. His pen gives birth to many successful books one after the other expanding the roots of his philosophy across the nation. The world takes the note of it. The many countries bestow upon him the greatest honors. He emerges as a worldly honored figure. The life at Anand Ashram and the wisdom of books makes him selfless person. He starts a self financed charitable trust with the commendable mission to reach to the rarest and distant part of the nation where the children are deprived of education and unable to pay for books. Through his self-financed charitable trust, he provides libraries to the senior citizens and old people living in Wrudha Ashram across the nation. He starts libraries in every nook and corner of the nation so that every child hungry for knowledge can easily reach to it and get the key to lead a sound, balanced and successful life, amalgamation of spiritual and material life.

The smell of his philanthropic mission crosses the frontiers of the nation and showering on him most covetous prizes and honour. Getting charmed with the charisma of Mr. Rajnandan, a delegation of most senior politicians of ruling political party reaches to him with a request and proposal that their party and of course the nation wants him to accept the honor of being the President of the nation. They further add that the nation wants to utilize his vision and his passion for the betterment of the nation. He feels happy that his mission is being loved and appreciated. Very humbly he refuses to accept it. He admits that it is his honor and greatness of the nation. He very candidly puts his philosophical argument that he has just come out of the charm, greed, and shining of material world and he does not wish to go back to it which deprives him and all the ignorant people who deprive themselves from the real pleasure of life by falling prey to the charm of material things in life. He expresses his fear and doubts that the hallow and charm of this greatest post would lead him back to that world where people remain starved for real food of their life.

He requests and appeals the delegations that if at all they want to honor him, then honor his last wish. Raising their eyebrows they humbly question him, "What is that?" Mr. Rajnandan says that he had made a great mistake in his life that he had kept himself and his family untouched from the books which teach the mankind the ways to be happy and real essence of human life. He humbly requests them that if possible they should take care that the bag of every learning child in the nation should have spiritual and religious books of the world. Let him study both. Presence of spiritual books along with the academics should be the part of the curriculum. If possible establish and start libraries in every distant nook and corner of the nation where the readers will get both material and spiritual enrichment. If it happened, he is sure that the coming generation will be a balanced generation and won't need to make extra efforts to find real pleasure in life i.e. peace of mind. The delegation gets enormously overwhelmed by this sacrificing, philosophical and philanthropic approach of Mr. Rajnandan. They become happy and leave the Anand Ashram of Mr. Rajnandan as if they have found the essence of life and a way to the success of the nation.

The next day all political parties meet and seriously consider the request of Mr. Rajnandan. They make a special provision in the nation's budget for starting libraries in every nook and corner of the nation. Unanimously they change the curriculum of all streams of education. They take care that the bag of every child going to school or a boy taking higher studies in senior institutes and universities should mark the presence of spiritual and religious books in it which would pave the way of balanced life for him and generations to come. When Mr. Rajnandan comes to know about the stand of the government he feels happy and takes out that book of the distant kinsman from the drawer stares at it for a while, kisses it and says "You made me happy gave me the real essence of life." The next morning he gets up and continues his mission with new inspiration and passion.

Dead Fish

It is the time to call a day. Dusk starts spreading its dark roof on the village, Hamidpur. But today's dusk seems to be somewhat different from its usual presence. It is not as animating and mirthful as it comes. It seems to be darker as if it is trying to cover some ominous thing in its dark and unfathomable womb. The presence of some evil thing in its dark womb makes it look somewhat gloomy and scaring as if it is strengthening the very popular saying 'bad events cast their shadows before'. It seems that dusk is giving the bell of happening of something ominous in the town of Hamidpur. A candle light is seen struggling to survive in the storm of darkness in the hut like house in one of the corners of the town. The exteriors and interiors of the house indicate that it might be a house of a peasant as the air in the house carries in it the smell of cow dung which troubles the nostrils. A blue light coming from oval shaped origins show that some cattle are tied in one corner of the house. In the middle of the house there is an open space where a wooden cot is kept. In darkness, it seems that there is a noisy wooden cot as two little children are making commotion on it. Suddenly a woman doing something in the dark corner of the house in the light of a candle addresses one of the children.

"Shrujan, your father has not come yet." Listening to his mother's voice, he tries to support her saying that he might be busy somewhere and assures her that he would be back soon and there is nothing to worry. She tells Shrujan that she is growing worried about his father and unwillingly reveals the reason behind her fear. She tells him that previous night, some hooligans had been to their house and abused his papa for interfering in the matters of the local M.L.A popularly known as Politician Mr. Sampatrao and warned his Papa if he does not stop opposing the Politician, they will see him. This scares her a lot. Seeing his mother in great concern little Shrujan holds her hand and tells her that there is no matter of worry and makes her realize that her mind is unnecessarily acting like a coward and it thinks too much. Little Shrujan advises her to have patience and tries to kill her fear positively saying that nothing wrong will happen. Her little son's words of advice give her some emotional relief and she goes back in the hut like house to finish the remaining work.

Mother's words about the men of the Politician make a permanent abode in the innocent mind of Shurjan. Suddenly he becomes silent as if he is brooding over the words of the men of the Politician. Lakshmi, Shrujan's little sister, disturbs his silent posture and questions him why is he silent? Shrujan says nothing and buries the fear of threat hidden in the words of the men of the Politician in deep corners of his mind and rejoins with his little sister, Lakshmi. Mother finishes her work and comes out closing her both the ears as if she is too much troubled by some cacophonous sound, to accompany the children lying on the wooden cot.

She tells little Shrujan that a bird has been hovering on their hut since long and his hovering is supposed to be bad omen. It troubles her a lot and enhances her fear. It is an ominous and more ominous when heard at this hour of eve. It is said and believed that the bird makes such sound when it anticipates about happening of some undesirable thing. Little Shrujan does not like her mother's argument and he reminds her that she is unnecessarily linking the late entry of his father with cacophonous sound of the bird. Mother nodding head negatively tries to convince him that evil sound of the bird has been responsible for the ruin of so many lives in the town and it is regarded as a sheer truth. Unconsciously she mutters as it has done with others it will do.........and comes back to her senses. Mother once again asks her little Shrujan that his father has not returned yet. Seeing his mother brooding over the issue of his father's not coming home, he prefers not to answer her this time and pretends that he is asleep. Little Shrujan is not mature enough to understand the concern which a woman or mother feels when her husband is away and does not inform her of his coming.

While lying on the wooden cot, her eyes catch a falling star and her doubt gets further strengthened. They don't understand the sleep overpowers them while waiting for the father. When their ears are disturbed by the crowing sound of the cock and twittering sounds of the birds around, they open their eyes to see that it is the time of morning and find that father has not returned home. Their concerns grow further.

A shepherd putting a black blanket on shoulders is going with his cattle to lush grooves on the bank of the river. While going, he finds that a body lying in the bushes on the bed of the river. He goes close and finds that it is of Shiripati fully drunk and unconscious. Instantly, the news gets spread in Hamidpur. A crowd rushes towards the spot and shifts the body of Shiripati to the civil hospital at Hamidpur. One of the gentlemen returns to intimate the family about the happening with Shiripati. The family too rushes to the civil hospital. Doctors make all possible efforts to save Shiripati but they fail. As the death is not natural and there are some doubtful conditions, the doctors perform the postmortem of Shiripati's body and conclude that poisonous wine caused his death.

Mother's doubt proves to be true. The bird, the gloomy dusk and the falling star predicted rightly. Mother goes back into past and remembers her husband Shripati who never touched wine.

Shiripati is an educated and successful farmer. He keeps good knowledge of Government schemes launched for the farmers, old people, orphans and widows. He introduces various government schemes which benefit a lot to the village. He makes the poor and illiterate rustics knowledgeable about the various government schemes such as subsidies for agriculture and monthly allowance of government for the women who are widows. In this way he serves his village and his work gives him good fame in the village. He has two acres of land beside the road located at the very entrance of Hamidpur. It is on this part of land, Mr. Sampatrao the fondly called 'Politician' casts his evil eyes. One day the Politician calls Shiripati puts the proposal for his land. He tells him that he wants to start a wine factory on this piece of land. Shiripati refuses the proposal saying that he does not want to contribute to the ruin of the families.

On hearing this reply, the Politician gets irritated at him and threatens him of losing life. Shiripati tells whole thing to his wife, alerts all the villagers from the evil intentions of the Politician which further intensifies the anger of the Politician. Shiripati's wife advises her husband to keep himself away from the Politician as it is not good for him and his family. But Shiripati pays not heed to this advice of his wife. One day when he is returning from his farm, the men of the Politician abduct and take to him to the bungalow of the Politician. He is kept foodless in a darkroom and late in the evening poisonous wine is poured into his mouth. At the early hours of the dawn, the body of Shiripati is thrown on the bed of river. Politician is a Politician.

Unexpected departure of Shiripati causes an irrevocable damage to the family. Survival in absence of the head of the family becomes a great challenge. Shrujan studying in the seventh standard is immature enough to lead a fatherless family. Shrujan's mother spends her sweat on the farm to survive her family during the worst time. All sources of financial incomes get blocked which make Shrujan to leave his education in middle. Adversities of the family reach its climax when little Lakshmi gets affected by cholera and economically harassed family can do nothing but to see the death of their darling daughter with their open eyes. Poor rain fall is being recorded for last several years which enhances the adversities of Shrujan's family. Endless worries bring flood of tears in the eyes of the family. Nothing comes out of the land. Shrujan's mother does some household jobs in the village and with great difficulties manages two times food.

Innocent Shrujan sees and equally bears the sufferings which caused due to the sudden demise of his father. Years pass, Shrujan grows and becomes twenty years old. Every year of life has significance as it shows how much he and his family suffered at the hands of destiny. Shrujan grows enough and his shoulder becomes strong enough to support the family of an old mother whose life is nothing but a life of suffering. To give a relief to her suffering mother, he begins to work as waiter in a wine shop in the town. One day, Shrujan is serving to a group of drunkards who claim them to be the men of Politician. They are uncontrolled and unknowingly open the history of the death of Shiripati which they had caused some years ago. One of them unconsciously reveals that how Shiripati was abducted and kept in the darkroom and forcefully poured poisonous alcohol into his mouth. He does not forget to reveal that they had done it at the instruction of Politician, Mr Sampatrao. Shrujan gets shocked to hear this truth behind his father's death.

Shrujan returns home, takes meal and lying on the wooden cot placed in the middle of the front yard thinks over the revelation of the drunkards in the bar. He becomes restless and determines that he would not leave the person who has made his family suffer a lot. He burns with anger and his soul flutters to take revenge on the Politician, Mr Sampatrao a man who caused the death of his father, who caused the death of his little sister Lakshmi, who caused unbearable suffering to his mother. Shrujan decides to give justice to his dead father and thinks that the Politician Mr. Sampatrao has no right to be happy. There is a huge bungalow of Sampatrao where he frequently comes.

One day Shrujan dares to enter his bungalow with a dagger from the backside balcony. Unfortunately when he tries to enter the bedroom where Sampatrao is lying accidently something falls down and the sound of that fallen thing makes Sampatrao alert. Shrujan anyhow succeeds in escaping from that hazardous situation and determines not to do such foolish adventure hereafter. He realizes that it is not possible to kill Sampatrao face to face as he being most influential political figure always surrounded by a crowd of activists and supporters. Every evening, after having meal, he rests on the wooden cot and looking at the stars in the sky, he tries to find a way to take revenge on his father's murderer. Suddenly an idea clicks to his mind "poison for poison"

Meanwhile Shrujan gives up the job in bear bar and joins a pharmaceutical unit of a company. It is here he acquires good knowledge of various medicines and poisonous chemicals. Once he secretly brings a bottle of poisonous chemical confirming it can cause death. After working for a few days there, he leaves that job and joins private hospital as an assistant of a doctor. This doctor once meets him in the company and from then they become good friends. It is in this hospital, Shrujan acquires the skill of how to inject a syringe. Secretly he manages to have some injections and keeps them in his hut. While doing this job in the hospital, he manages the time to keep watch on activities on the bungalow of Politician. He keeps a serious watch on the coming and going of the Politician. During his watch, he observes that Mr. Sampatrao comes on every Sunday to stay at the bungalow in Hamidpur and rest of the days he spends in Mumbai. It is on every Sunday; Shrujan visits the canteen which is in front of the bungalow of the Politician spends some time taking tea. He observes that every Sunday the driver of Sampatrao goes to the market carrying a cloth bag.

One day he decides to chase the driver to see where the driver goes. He finds that the driver visits the shop of a woman who sells fish. He makes this observation number of times. Meanwhile, Shrujan visits that woman's shop pretending to be a customer. One day he asks the woman about the driver. The woman unknowingly reveals him that he is the driver of Mr. Sampatrao and he comes to take fish for his master. She further adds that the driver comes on every Sunday. Frequent visits to the shop of the woman enable Shrujan to have good relation with her. He decides to exploit this relationship. Once he reveals her that he has no job and adds how his family is going through the adversities. The woman takes pity on him and offers him a job of bringing fish from the dealer. Shrujan happily accepts this job. Every day he goes to dealer to bring fish. After coming from there he uses the remaining time to help the woman in handling the customers. He anxiously waits for every Sunday because it is on every Sunday the driver comes there. Sincerity of Shrujan wins the trust of the fisherwoman. The day of revenge comes. Shrujan takes bottle of poison and syringes. He loads that syringe with poisonous chemical. As usual he goes to the dealer to bring fish. While coming, he stops at place and puts down the basket of fish. He takes out some large size fish and injects poisonous chemicals into them. When the driver of the Politician comes, the woman asks Shrujan for fresh fish of larger size. Shrujan very skillfully offers her the fish injected with poisonous chemicals. The woman takes fish and cuts them into smaller pieces. The driver as usual pays the bill takes the fish home. The next day, Shrujan happens to see the photograph of the Politician, Mr. Sampatrao and reads the news of sudden demise of the Politician.

Shrujan brings the news paper home and shows it to his suffering mother. After seeing the photograph and reading the matter written under, she smiles at Shrujan. After having meal with his mother Shrujan goes to bed and enjoys such sound and thoughtless slumber which he could never have previously.

Life Survived and
Death...............Postponed

There is a dilapidated haveli like structure at the outskirt of the town, Sundar Nagar. It has been a long deliberately ignored and isolated part of Sundar Nagar as the dilapidated haveli like structure exists with its mysterious past. Scaring rumors about the age old haveli have been deeply rooted in the culture and life of the people living in Sundar Nagar. It is out of this long rooted scare and mysterious conditions in the haveli, people prefer to be away from this decaying structure and never allow their children and other members of the family to visit that structure or go there on any other cause. Thus, this haveli has been leading a silent life for many decades.

For many years, the interiors of the haveli have not felt the presence of any human being. Nor any human or non human sound could disturb the silent interiors of the Haveli. In ancient times Renowned Nawabs and their dynasties ruled this haveli and now what rules it is a grave silence where human beings fear to go. It seems that every day dawns on Sundar Nagar purposefully excluding the dilapidated haveli. For the first time since a long period, it seems that, the day has dawned on the decaying haveli. It has brought it into light and dared to disturb the long ruling silence with an arrival of a pregnant bitch that gives birth to four robust and charming puppies. The noisy presence of the puppies have shaken the very roots of the silence which thought herself to be an unconquered queen of this ancient structure.

Coming and going out of the haveli in search of food for herself and her puppies has been a daily routine of the bitch. In the absence of the mother, naughty puppies loiter in all the isolated dark corners of the haveli and sometimes they dare to go up on the ceilings of the haveli and make barking like sounds so that the world outside would take note of their presence. The sound of the puppies has succeeded in arresting the attention of the natives of the Sundar Nagar. When the bitch returns to the haveli, the puppies jump on her to suck milk. There is a rivalry among them to suck more milk. Happy days of the puppies just go on passing and it seems that haveli too is enjoying the happy company of the noisy and naughty puppies.

One day, the bitch comes at the afternoon and feeds the puppies and goes out in Sundar Nagar for her work. It is too late in the evening; the bitch doesn't come back to the haveli. The puppies are anxiously waiting for their mother and never thought that they would never meet their mother hereafter. Whole night the puppies pass by making loud barking sound and eventually they go to bed with hope that their mother would return tomorrow morning and satisfy their hungry stomach. The day dawns and gradually the sun starts peeping through the decaying ceilings of the haveli yet, the bitch doesn't return to the haveli. The puppies decide to go out in Sundar Nagar to find out their mother. All the puppies leave the haveli handing over the reins of the haveli to queen silence once again. They leave the haveli with hungry stomachs and get separated never to come together again.

The story of sudden departure of the bitch is revealed by one of the old gentlemen in town that Nagar Panchayat had undertaken the campaign of trapping the mad dogs and troubling dogs. Accidently or unknowingly the campaigners caught the bitch along with other mad dogs and took them away for further procedure. One of the puppies goes quite deep into lanes of Sundar Nagar and takes a pause at a huge bungalow. He gets enchanted by the beautiful exteriors of the bungalow and hopes that he would get something to eat here. The puppy dares to peep through the slightly open iron gate of the bungalow and sees that a beautiful girl is playing with her dancing doll in the front yard of the bungalow. The name of this girl is Rupa and she is beautiful like her name. While playing, she smells the presence of a cotton like creature standing at the gate as if he is giving a standing ovation to his new mistress. Rupa gets so much attracted towards this puppy and hurriedly she runs towards him and picks him, caresses him, takes him in and offers him some milk and food. Puppy becomes happy with the idea that he has got his caretaker.

Gradually Puppy succeeds in making special place for himself in the household of Rupa. All the members of the family love him and care him. They also organize a naming ceremony to name this Puppy. Unanimously they decide to call him by the name 'Tommy'. Tommy becomes his identity and very soon he becomes one of the members of the family. The family becomes so habitual with his presence that slight absence of Tommy in the household marked with special and keen attention by all. He becomes a darling to all. When the father of Rupa returns from the office in the evening, he plays mischief with him by going through his legs making a little bit calmer barking sound. When Rupa's father is lying on the bed after having meal, he sits beside the father and cleans his heels with his tongue as if he is paying respect to his master. When mother is in the kitchen, Tommy goes and holds her sari with his teeth and brings her in drawing room to play. Mother too develops an affinity with this little puppy. For Rupa, Tommy becomes a great companion. When Rupa is doing her studies, Tommy just sits beside her carefully sees what Rupa does. If any stranger knocks at the gate, Tommy goes and starts barking at him and prevents him from coming in. Playing with Rupa at the time of dusk is a great pastime for him. He misses her very much when she is in the school or away from him on account of any cause. When Rupa returns from the school in the evening, the first thing she does is that she straightly goes to Tommy and picks him up and kisses and caresses him. After having tea, Rupa and Tommy come out in the front yard to play. Chasing each other and playing hide and seek game are their favorite games. Sometimes Rupa chases him and sometimes Tommy does in return. During hide and seek game Tommy runs through the trees and bushes of the front and back yard of the bungalow and Rupa chases to find him out. They enjoy this game very much. It becomes their evening ritual and both cannot live without it. When the time of going to bed comes, Tommy instantly takes his position on the bed just beside his loving mistress.

One day, when Rupa is chasing Tommy in hide and seek game, Tommy secretly runs through the bushes of the backyard hiding himself behind and through the bushes he comes to the front yard. Till now Tommy's life is confined in the interiors of the huge bungalow of Rupa. After seeing the main gate slightly open, he runs so quickly like blowing stormy wind through the gate and pierces through the gap between the front and back tires of a fully loaded truck. While chasing Tommy, Rupa arrives at the gate and sees Tommy piercing through the gap between the tires as if a speedy arrow pierces through its hard target. Rupa gets shocked and her whole body starts trembling with fear. She closes her eyes with sweaty palms and just imagines the picture which would be before her on the very next moment. She cannot bear that scenario with a lot of spreading blood and scattered pieces of Tommy's cotton like body. Tears are about to fall and the whole face of Rupa becomes pale and scared unwillingly she starts sliding down the curtain of the palms which would have prevented her from seeing and witnessing the most ominous scene which she never thought of. Palms slide down gradually and Rupa slowly opens her eyes to see undesirable things happened. The fully loaded truck runs over a little Tommy but leaves him uninjured. Tommy reaches to such portion of the road between the front and back tires where nothing could harm him. Out of fear he shrinks his whole body and sits down with fear at the middle of the road. Within no time, the loaded truck runs over him untouched. Thus he gets escaped from the impending disaster. When Rupa opens her eyes, she gets shocked and felt on the top of the air to see that Tommy is quite safe and sitting at the middle of the road as if a sage is doing penance for years.

The tears rolling out of her eyes change its tragic colors and within no time turned out to be the tears of happiness. Rupa wasting not a single moment rushes towards him and picks him up and kisses him hundred times and caresses him releases a puff of air which says Life Survived and Death---------Postponed.

Rupa takes Tommy in hurriedly and narrates the whole incident to her parents. They get thrilled and instantly decide to appoint a gate security to avoid the unexpected exits of Tommy and recurrence of such ominous events which may cause a threat to the life of their darling cotton like creature.

A Smile Takes Life

It is a cold dawn at the mid of December when Shrungarpur a small town is in its sound slumber. Since it is the mid of December, the bitter chill of the winter is spitting out its chill fire on the people of Shrungarpur. People are seen confined and struggling to get warm in their blankets. Little kids embrace their mothers to get some warm. Elderly gentlemen are sleeping in the front yards of their houses and struggling in their blankets to protect themselves from the blow of bitter chill. Cattle are tied to the wooden sticks fixed deep into the ground and standing still with closing eyes and shrinking their bodies to protect them from the bitter chill of winter. A fluttering sound of a flag accompanied by a sound of a musical performance happening in the sanctum of the temple falls on the ear. Gradually, the sun comes out in the sky to lessen the intensity of the cold fire of winter and makes the whole town of Shrungarpur feel at warm and comfortable from the bitter blows of the cold. The elderly people end their bhajans and kirtanas in the temple and come out of the temple to reach to their homes. While coming out of temple, all the old gentlemen are engrossed in their discussion. It is heard from one of them saying that for the first time after a long period, they have experienced and felt such cold winter season. They are so engrossed in their talk and hurry to reach to their homes to begin their daily routine that they don't pay heed to who are around them. There is a little open space covered from up by the ceiling of the temple where a man like figure is at rest. His body movements show that he too is suffered the blows of the cold and is trying to shrink his whole body in the tattered clothes that he has worn. He is none other than the only and lonely beggar of the town. He has grown a long beard and long uncombed dirty hair. His clothes are dirty and torn and his appearance is such that no one likes to see him or entertain him a while. But the beggar is careless of the treatment of the people and happy in his profession of beggary.

The beggar is in his mid thirties. He has been a part of Shrugarpur for many years. He begins his day by visiting shops and houses in the town and whatever the eatables he gets from the housewives, he gathers in his dirty and tattered cloth bag and comes out of the town where there is a small temple of some god where he takes his food and remaining he offers to the dogs who gather there with the hope that the beggar may bring some new and tasty food for them. After gathering food from the people, he prefers to lead his life in isolation at the small deserted temple outside the town. He does it because he does not want that people of Shrungarpur should scorn at him or make him a subject of fun and mockery.

Every day he gets enough money along with eatables. Only ten rupees out of the collected amount he keeps in his pocket. A question may be raised what does he do with the rest of the gathered money? The answer is just behind this deserted temple where there is a little open space. It is here, the beggar makes a deep ditch in which he keeps his remaining money. After burying his money in this ditch he keeps a small stone on it as a mark of identification. The place is quite safe as no one comes to this temple and there is no fear of its being stolen.

There is a huge edifice at the center of Shrungarpur. It is really a huge and attractive one. Everyone in the town aspires to have such luxurious house for himself. It is the edifice of a rich Landlord of the town. The Landlord exercises a good influence on the people of Shrugarpur. It is said about the rich Landlord that he is arrogant and takes great pride in his affluence. His affluence has made him so proud that he avoids talking to the people who are lower to him in class and prosperity. He prefers to have relations with the people who are of his status. Only rich people in and out of Shrugarpur are seen going in and coming out of his splendid edifice. Entry of the common and poor people is strictly prohibited. If any one does, he has to hear a lot of shouting and abuses. So common people prefer to keep themselves away from the edifice and enjoy its glory from a safer distance. When its so, there is no question of entry of the beggars who for them nothing but an insult and disgrace to the society.

When the beggar is resting in the isolated temple, his eyes catch a huge tower like edifice of the rich Landlord. It seems to him that the huge edifice is calling him for handsome offerings. During his walk in the town, he has heard about the arrogance and the treatment that the rich Landlord gives to people. It is out of this impression; he deliberately keeps himself away from the charm of the edifice. Whenever he rests in that isolated temple and looks at the huge edifice, his expectation becomes stronger and allurement of handsome offering becomes so strong that he cannot control himself and falls prey to the allurement and glory of the edifice of the Landlord. One day he musters his courage and decides to visit the edifice. He goes quite close to the edifice but after seeing an alert security guard who is smoking and releasing smoke up in the air, he changes his mind with the anticipation that security guard may be harsh to him.

A few days later, when he is passing by the lane where the grand bungalow of the landlord is located marks the absence of the security guard and finds that the huge iron gate is slightly open. Taking the advantage of the absence of the security guard, he dares to open the gate and enters. At that moment the Landlord is deeply engaged in washing his favorite car. After seeing the beggar is entering his bungalow, Landlord hurriedly comes there and exchanges a few harsh words.

"Who is there trespassing my territory? Don't you know here common and dirty pigs from nasty mud are strictly prohibited?" Over this the beggar says, "Sorry! Sir." Landlord shouts at him, "Haven't you read the message out there?" The beggar says in a low voice, "No Sir. I forgot." Landlord asks angrily, "What brings you here?" In reply Beggar humbly says, "I have a great fascination for your edifice and have the hope that man who owns such huge edifice how magnanimous he would be at heart! Expecting a handsome offering from you, I dared to come in." Landlord says rather irritatingly, "stop your baffling and putting me on pedestal. Your words of flattery will not change my mind. Don't stop here for a single moment you 'Nasty Pig' from mud. Your dirty presence has spoiled the beauty and glory of my huge edifice. Get out of my sight instantly otherwise you will pay for your misdeed." Beggar bows down, tears begins to flow from his eyes. He looks at the Landlord with a feeling of being insulted. He wants to speak further but holds his tongue back. Looking angrily at the beggar, the Landlord warns him rather harshly and inhumanly, "Don't dare to have an eye on grand edifice hereafter. Take care in future that your nasty legs should not move towards my edifice. Your presence is nothing but a disgrace to me and people like me in the town. Beggar felt very sorry over what he did and begging him says, "Sorry! Sir I will take absolute care of it." He leaves the bungalow dishearteningly.

The word 'Nasty Pig' troubles him a lot. He decides and determines that whatever may happen he would never come here for begging where there is Landlord's edifice. A long period of 20 years or more is passed. The beggar has reached in his fifties. These twenty years proved very hard for the Landlord. These are the years of lot of happenings in the life of Landlord. He has a lonely son who spoils his life by joining the company of drunkards. He drinks and drinks until the wine drinks him. One day his son returns to the edifice in drunken state and falls ill. He has become so thin and pale that he cannot wake up. The Landlord uses the power of money invites doctors to cure him. Doctors tell him that his son's kidneys are damaged. One doctor gives him a suggestion of Kidney transplant. For the love of his lonely son, he takes the suggestion of the doctor. The drinking addict and now kidney transplantation puts the Landlord in a great financial trouble. His son has already wasted a lot of property on his addicts and what left is his huge edifice. Finally, the Landlord makes up his mind and makes the auction of his pride i.e. edifice. Taking money, he reaches to hospital and requests the doctor to complete the process of transplantation. The process is done, but it proves to be fatal to the life of the son and during treatment, the son loses his life. The Landlord is sunk in despair. He brings back the dead body of son and does the cremation and remaining rituals after the death of his son. Within a few days, Landlord's wife can not bear the shock of her son's death and she too dies out of heart failure. Landlord goes on bearing severe blows of the destiny one after the other. First he lost his huge edifice then he lost his son and now his wife. He becomes absolutely bankrupt. What remains with the Landlord is nothing. His situation becomes so worse that he has to take a small room on rent in Shrungarpur where he spends remaining life.

It is the habit of the beggar that whatever the amount of money he gathers in a day, he keeps only ten rupees out it in his pocket and remaining he buries in the ditch behind the deserted temple where he spends his time. The question comes in one's mind what does he do with that ten rupees? Every evening, the beggar goes in Shrungarpur to collect his evening food. There is a row of shops just beside the main temple of Shrungarpur. One of the shops is a lottery stall named Mahalakshim Lottery Center. When it is too late in evening and the market of Shrungapur is about to get closed and when people are dispersing towards their homes, the beggar secretly goes to the lottery shop and takes a lottery ticket of ten rupees. He has been doing it since last twenty years. One day he returns to his deserted temple to take rest and gets shocked to see that his treasure has been stolen by somebody. He feels very disappointed and on the very next moment a question encourages and boosts his morale that why a beggar needs so much money. Beggar is beggar and he should be happy with two times meals. Fortunately, it is on the same day his fortune smiles upon him and his ticket wins a lottery worth amount ten crore. Beggar becomes rich overnight. He uses that amount to build a huge edifice like that of the Landlord. Now, the beggar has become the most affluent and respectable person in the town of Shrungarpur. Beggar is completely ignorant to the lot of the Landlord and he too does not know about the beggar's achievement as he engaged in the treatment of his drunkard son.

One day the Landlord is passing by the road suddenly takes a pause at an edifice which resembles like him. He throws a glance at in and finds that rich man is washing his car. Accidently or by chance the eyes of both the rich beggar and the poor Landlord catch each other. The rich beggar looks at the Landlord identifies him and smiles at him innocently. The Landlord cannot bear this smile and hurriedly comes to his rented room and locks himself in. The next morning the whole Shrugarpur rushes towards the room where the landlord lives as a tenant. The police come and break the door which is locked within and bring out the dead body of the poor Landlord. Police register it to be the case of suicide. Police find a piece of paper in the room of the landlord on which it is written 'A 'Smile' took my life.'

The School for the Thieves

The world of evil is getting up to raise its head up and to let loose its anarchic forces to disturb the peace of the world which is asleep and dreaming of colorful tomorrow with falling and spreading darkness over the town of Bairagpur. It is the town where it becomes difficult to make distinction between a thief and a gentleman as the most of the people in the town are the thieves of all kind on the record of the police station. Most of them are notorious as burglar, pickpocket, mugger, and shoplifter. Like men, one gets confused in locating the houses of the gentlemen and the thieves. So Bairagpur is nothing but a sludge of chaos as Bairagpur has two separate identities good for day and bad for the night. It is highly sensitive and hoodwinking town as its so called gentleman becomes an ardent thief with falling darkness. Arrival of a patrolling van either at the day time or late in the night in search of their food has become an integral part of routine life of the town. Interesting thing of the thieves of the town is that sometimes they attack on each other's house. The cacophonous and equally terrifying sound of the patrolling police van has become so common to the people and especially to the little kids and crying babies that they enjoy it as a play toy.

It is on one rainy night, the stepping sound of a dark figure disturbs the placidity of darkness. When the showering like rain falls on the raincoat of dark figure and when the person goes through the light of a dim street light, it shines like silver stream. The face of the dark figure becomes unidentifiable as its face is almost eclipsed by the dark shadow of raincoat's cap. All of a sudden, the sound of patrolling van disturbs and fears manly stepping of the dark figure. He moves with a fright of being caught and takes shelter behind the backside wall of a house. The police van goes ahead but seems to be stopped at a close distance. The dark figure, controlling his scared breath, tries to move his head to see and confirm whether the van has gone but he becomes more alert after seeing the police van is stopped at a calling distance and that some police men are engaged in an enquiry with a person. The dark figure wants to hide him at a secure place but finds no place. The backside wall where he is hiding himself has a window which is open and throws the light outside through the iron bars of the window. The dark figure plans to break the bars and rob the house. When he peeps through the window, the inside scenario moves his heart and helplessly he has to go back from his intention. The scenario transforms him thoroughly. This flint hearted Thief becomes emotional for the first time in his life. He sees that a long waiting and hungry mother and her little son are engaged in a talk, the sound of which falls on the ear of the Thief hiding behind the house.

The little boy asks his mother, "Mummy, where is my father? You told me that he has gone to do the theft and would bring bread for me. Mummy, I have been hungry for the last two days and hunger has become so unbearable that I feel that I will die if I don't get food." It makes her emotional and hiding her tearful eyes, she convinces him. "My darling, my dear little child your father is great thief and I am sure that he will come shortly with lot of food." To this the boy replies "Really! Is my father a great thief? Mother a little bit proudly answers, "Yes my dear child." In order to divert the attention of the child from hunger she questions him. "My dear son what will you do, when you will be a grown up person?" To this boy boastingly, ignorantly and innocently answers, "Mummy! I will be a great thief like my father." Happy mother with this answer gives a pat on the back of her little son.

This brief talk moves the Thief's heart but makes him ironically laugh at himself for he as a thief is planning to rob the house of the another thief. Suddenly the angry steeping sound of the police march towards the house where the thief is hiding. He shrinks and gets alert. The police men knock at the door of the house. Expecting that her husband would be there, the woman opens the door and gets shocked and worried seeing the Police there outside. They break the news that her husband has been killed by an angry mob when he had been caught while robbing a house. They inform her that the dead body of her thief husband has been at their disposal at the police station and she has to collect it tomorrow morning. After breaking this news, the Police disappear living woman in an almost collapsed state. The woman cannot bear this shock and falls on the ground never to get up. Seeing his mother lying on the ground, the little boy wails loudly. "Mummy, get up! Mummy, get up! Why are you lying down and not speaking to me? I am hungry and you promised for food." The wails of the little boy grow louder. The Thief enters through the main door and lifts the baby leaving the dead mother there only anticipating that the police may come tomorrow and take her body for further process.

The Thief gets moved by the condition of the boy. He picks him up and takes him to his house where he is staying with his wife who suffers from a childless situation. They had got married ten years back yet they don't have children of their own. When the Thief narrates the state of affairs in the room where he had planned to rob, the thief's wife too gets moved by the bad luck of the child. Both are happy as for the first time after their marriage, the cry of child has shaken the barren silence of their house. Thief's wife is so happy that she feels that the boy is none other than her own son. The coming of the boy adds colors in the life of the Thief's family. They call him by the name Raviraj. The wife of the Thief becomes so habitual with him that she cannot imagine and bear a single moment's absence of Raviraj. Whole day she goes on fondly uttering only one name that is Raviraj.

Raviraj grows and with passing time, the memories of his real mother and father grow dimmer and dimmer. He becomes almost oblivion of them except a word which gets inscribed on the slate of his memory and starts assuming that thief and his wife are his parents. One day Thief returns home and finds that the engaged wife in the kitchen is unable to pay heed at the crying Raviraj. He holds him up and places him on the cot and puts some toys around him so that he can play with them. The Thief begins questioning him. "Dear Ravi, "What would you like to be in future?" Ravi instantly replies, "A great thief." The Thief takes it to be quite positively. The Thief curiously questions him, "Would you like to learn the art of theft?" Ravi positively nods. The Thief conveys his agreement saying that he would make him a great thief. Ravi becomes extremely happy with this and he gets prepared himself to be the great thief. Ravi is too little and immature to understand who is called a thief and what does a theft mean? He is so innocent that he is unable to understand the evilness of the concept of a 'Thief'. He takes it quite easily and finds a fun in saying that he wants to be a great thief.

The Thief admits him in a school. On the very first day of the school, the Thief brings some books for Ravi. On the eve of the first day of Ravi's school, the Thief sits beside Ravi and tells him that the he is going to teach him how to be a great thief. Little and curious Ravi with great interest sits beside the Thief. Before dealing with the books, he explains to Ravi the concept of theft in the fewest possible and easy words. He tells him that the theft is nothing but entering in someone's house and taking things hidden either in the cupboard or suitcase or some locked objects and taking them to our house. He tells him putting a book of English rhymes in front of him, "Imagine that this book is a nothing but a house of some one. If you want see what is there in the house, the thief questions Ravi what will you do?" To this little Ravi brilliantly answers, "I will open the book." The thief encourages him saying that "That is like a good boy." The thief reads out a poem and asks him to read it now and intentionally tells him that while reading, he has to steal the words or lines from the poem and store them in his mind which is nothing but his house where he hides the things that he has stolen. To make it easier, the Thief explains to him briefly, the book is the house of someone. The poems or lesson in the book is treasure of the owner. To have this treasure, one has to go in and pick up the valuable things and come back to one's house where he can hide the stolen things.

After a few days practice, the boy acquires the skill of the theft. He is so innocent and ignorant to understand the darker side of the theft and applies the theory of theft to books only. His passion for encroaching into the periphery of the books enhances. Realizing this, the Thief too brings new books for him every day from the market and adds fuel to the burning desire of the child to be a great thief. Whenever, the Thief and Ravi sit together, the Thief questions what he stole yesterday. Ravi then proudly presents before him some words or some lines of the rhymes from the book.

With growing time, Ravi too grows, going from one standard to the other. In the course of the time he attains that much maturity to distinguish between the good and bad theft. He thinks that the earlier is the best for him and thanks the thief to whom he regards his real father for teaching him the art of doing the good theft. Thief and wife are quite happy to see that their son Ravi marching on the track which they decided for him. Ravi grows, completes his education joins as a professor in a college. But very soon he gets fed up with the working conditions there and eventually he quits the job. A thought to start his own school fans his imagination. He puts the proposal before the Thief to which the Thief responds quite positively.

Very soon, Ravi starts his school to which he names Raviraj Institutions which becomes so popular that every parents wants his ward to be admitted in Raviraj Institutions. Considering the demand of the Parents and a long list of the waiting students, Raviraj introduces new institutes. Every coming year goes on adding new schools and colleges to the Raviraj Institutions. Very soon Raviraj institutions become the topmost and highly preferred educational institute in the state making its owner means Raviraj economically very sound person. Considering the growing burden of the responsibilities, the Thief too takes active participation in the institute's administration and tries to lessen the burden of responsibility of his son.

The Thief never opens the chapters of history of Raviraj and tells him the bitter truth of his family back ground. He also deliberately hides from him what he used to do to feed Raviraj and family. He does so because he is afraid that Raviraj may develop an inferiority complex or negative approach towards himself and his family. Thus the Thief keeps him away from the evil spell of his and Raviraj's real father's profession.

Once it happens that Raviraj and the Thief are meeting the desirous and ambitious parents who wish to have their wards admitted in the Raviraj institutions. There comes a widow with her son aspiring to take admission for Engineering in Raviraj institutions. Conversation begins; woman presents a few pages of her life history and the cause of her family tragedy. When Raviraj comes to know that she is a widow of a gangster who was recently encountered for his anti-social activities, the first thing he does that he asks her son to go out for sometime and then tells the woman very proudly, that in our institute children of rich class take education. If their parents come to know about the presence of a son having criminal background, they may object. He too expresses a fear that the presence of such students in his institute may have an adverse impact on the future of his institutions. So he very rudely denies the request of the widow. On this woman gets irritated and boldly questions Raviraj, "Does it mean that the children having criminal background have no right to get educated? Does it mean that they should not be given a chance to wipe out the disgrace on their families? Denying admission to my son, does it mean that you don't want to give them a chance to amend and be back to the main stream of the society?" The Thief was patiently listening to the arguments of the widow but prefers to keep quite as he does not want to interfere in the business of his son. Perhaps he is afraid that his interference may not be tolerated.

Raviraj gets annoyed at these aggressive arguments of the woman and tells her that he cannot give admission to her son in his institute. Woman keeps quiet and leaves the cabin. Immediately after the departure of the woman, the Thief helplessly interferes and asks his son Raviraj what would have been wrong, if he had been given admission. On this Raviraj poses the prestige issue and tells him that he does not do such things which can hamper the name and progress of the institute. So far the Thief has held his tongue back but seeing the scenario in the cabin and the begging of the woman, the Thief helplessly lets loose his tongue and gets involved in a hectic argument with Raviraj, "My dear son, you have done a wrong thing, it is an injustice to woman and her innocent son." To this Raviraj says, "My stand was right, father." The Thief says, "Do you mean that they are faulty for having criminal background?" Raviraj irritatingly replies, "I don't want to get involved in deciding who is right and who is wrong? What matters for me is the future of mine and my institutions." The Thief questions, "What will happen to all those children whose parents are either thieves or involved in some antisocial activities?" Warning Raviraj of the consequences of his action, Thief says, "If they are not educated and given a chance to be back in the main stream of the society, they will follow the foot prints of their parents and history will be repeated. Do you want this to happen?" To this Raviraj replies rather practically, "My dear father I am completely a professional person. I am not a social worker to have sympathy for these people for me they are nothing but a disgrace to the society. It is just because of such a few people, the entire society suffers and eventually gets defamed. It is better if they dissociate themselves from such people who are nothing but a headache."

Anger of the Thief reaches at its extreme on seeing his son has grown sufficiently professional, materialistic and listless to the emotions of the sufferers. He continues his argument and fearlessly uncovers the truth of his life fully anticipating its consequences. He says, "My dear son, Raviraj, I am not your father. Your father was a thief and he was murdered by an angry crowd when he was doing a theft. It was I taking pity on your miserable condition brought you my home and made you what you are today." It is the expectation of the Thief after that hearing this record of his life, Raviraj may change its philosophical stand but happens completely contrary. To this Raviraj replies, "Now it does not matter to me whether I was a son of a thief or a sadhu. Whatever you did is really a great thing and thanks for goodness."

Getting extremely annoyed at Raviraj, he questions him very aggressively, "If there is no place to the son of an evil person in your institutions, it is better not to imagine about the place of a thief in your life." To this Raviraj scornfully replies, "I and thief cannot go together." The Thief gets frustrated and determines not to spend a single moment there.

He returns home packs his luggage and returns to his native. He feels very sad at the fact despite of being educated; the people make distinction between good and bad. He exclaims, "If all are treated equally, this distinction won't exist!" On the very next moment, he realizes that the world survives on this distinction, and nobody wants to end it as it's end will end their interest. The Thief develops great commiseration for this deprived, unnoticed section of the society and dies to do something so that the disgrace of being a member of thief community would be erased and all will get equal right to grow and develop in their lives.

The Thief gets disheartened by this cool reply of his son who has grown inhuman in the race of earning his livelihood. The Thief feels sad at heart and gets disheartened by the thought that his teaching has gone in vain. Thief being financially sound, he takes step ahead and dares to start a school for the thieves. To which he names as "The School for the Thieves." On the very opening day of the school, he feels pleasantly shocked to see a long queue of parents with their children representing the evil section of the world. Parents are seen expressing the satisfaction that finally they have got a place where their children will not be distinguished. A separated group of the parents is seen engrossed in reading a long caption written in bold letters displayed especially on the separated portion of the school. "The children of burglars, pickpockets, muggers, and shoplifters, chain grabbers, murderers, rapists, terrorists, hooligans and all other members of the evil society are allowed."

The Thief becomes happy with the way the school is flourishing and devotes rest of his life for exterminating the distinction between the evil and good which are nothing but offspring of the so called selfish society.

As You Sow, So You Reap

It is the morning time. Most of the shops on the ever busy Kasturba Gandhi road in Barahanpur are yet to open. It is the time when the city experiences dying silence as the caravan of the vehicles with their cacophonous sounds are slowly coming to perform on this road. It is the most favorite road for the people of Barahanpur as the most of the shops of luxuries and comforts are situated on this road and it is only road in the city which provides all sorts of needs of the people and thus no one returns home empty handed. For the food lovers, the Kasturba Gandhi road is a favorite place as it has all kinds of food stalls and hawkers who please the taste of their ever demanding tongue. At the evening time, the road takes the form of the fair as if the entire Barahanpur has come there for merry making. It is the most preferred place for clandestine meeting of isolated lovers. A good number of hospitals are situated on this road and most of them record tremendous rush of the patients as they have won the trust of the people with their caring and loving approach. Almost all the hospitals survive well except one which is named as Uday Hospital. There is 'rise' in its meaning but it seems that it has never seen its 'Uday'. The hospital started five years before but since its foundation, it seldom experiences the presence of the patients. It might be the reason why the hospital building takes a murky look.

In other hospitals, the patients have to wait for the doctors but in Uday hospital it is the doctor who has to wait for the patients. Due to this poor response of the patients, all the things in the hospital put on a gloomy look. If anyone enters the hospital, he may get the impression that the hospital is yet to be touched by the human presence. Interiors and the beds of the patients are so unclean that it compels one to think that the doctor who runs this hospital may not be in a position to spend on the hygienic conditions of the hospital. A compounder is sitting on the chair. His physical appearance shows that he has been fed up with this job as if he has never got an opportunity to serve the patient. All the things from the color of the walls to the colors of the flowers in the flower vase seem to be colorless. There is an isolated cabin where the doctor sits. The cabin too has a dull look waiting long for renovation. It is the cabin of the doctor and the wooden name plate on the dusty table shows that it is of Dr. Shrinivasan. Suddenly the compounder sitting on the table stands at his place as a part of respect to his arriving master. Dr. Shrinivasan hurriedly enters his cabin as if he has been late and there is a long queue of patients waiting for him. The compounder instantly goes in and puts the news paper on the table so that he can engage himself with that. Dr. Shrinivasan says to his compounder, "Mahesh, has anyone come?" Mahesh instead of giving an oral response and hurting his master, he prefers to convey negation by nodding gesture. His nodding saying 'No' troubles the doctor a lot. He puts down the paper and gets engrossed in looking above as if a huge question is troubling him. Dr. Shrinivasan remains in the same posture for a very long time. The increasing hours of the day enhance his boredom and anxiety. His fresh face of morning turns pale and futureless. Till the late afternoon, he waits for the patients but no hope comes in his way and he gets sunk in despair. The compounder brings his tiffin box kept in his bike's dickey. After serving his lunch, Mahesh retires for his daily ritual (taking lunch then a nap). The lunch taken by Doctor is so heavy that he starts snoring in the chair itself. When they get up they find that it is five o' clock.

They refresh themselves and again sit on their thrones hopefully waiting for the patients. But none comes there. Dr. Shrinivasan irritatingly gets up and leaves the cabin asking Mahesh to wind up. This has been the routine of Dr. Shrinivasan and the compounder Mahesh. A patient or two rarely comes there which keeps the doctor and his compounder alive. Whenever a patient comes in his hospital, the doctor charges him very heavily and prescribes him unnecessary but harmless tablets which give him some commission. As a result of this, the patient does not revisit his hospital. Thus the things grow worse raising a big question mark on the survival of the doctor and the people depend on him.

The next day when he returns to the hospital, he finds an envelope placed on his table. Curiously he opens it but gets shocked to see it to be a notice of the building owner in which he runs his hospital. He reads out the letter with a furrowed face which states that the rent of the last three months has been unpaid. If not paid within two months, he will have to leave the building. The message in the letter not only horrifies him but steals his sleep. It steals his enthusiasm and makes him frustrated with the question how to overcome the concern. Whole day he spends sitting in the concerned chair and hopelessly staring at the ceiling of the cabin. But no solution could strike to his mind. With great irritation, he leaves the cabin asking the compounder to shut down. The concerns of survival not only rule in the hospital but also they begin to knock door of his house. Coincidentally, it is on the same day, his wife receives a letter from the school where his son is studying. Dr. Shrinivasan's wife hands over the letter to her husband. He opens it and begins to read. As he begins to read the letter, the furrows on his face get dark and darker and his face turn watery. He takes out handkerchief to wipe out the sweat on his face. His wife understands and wants to speak but seeing his tense mood, she silences her tongue and waits for him to begin. Looking at her with a somewhat concerned and frustrated face he addresses his wife, "Sareeta, the days are growing hostile to me. Business at the hospital is almost dead. Expenses are ceaselessly growing with no income. I do nothing but hopelessly wait for the patients who ultimately deceive me. I want to do some business to survive but my qualification and my dignity come in the way. I am want of other skills which can empower me in these weakening circumstances. I am really fed up with these never ending things of concern. Survival has become really a great problem. I am fed up with my dead business and the hospital building owner with me. I don't understand how to solve the riddle of this troubled life. If possible suggest me. I am really ready to accept anyone's suggestion if it takes me out of these troubled conditions."

He speaks, speaks and suddenly turns silent. Sareeta understands his worries and his state of mind. In a soft and humble tone she asks him, "Won't you get hurt, if I dare to suggest you?" Hopefully looking at her he says, "No dear! Not in any way. You have been a well wisher of mine and won't mind if you suggest me." Sareeta suggests him, "Why don't you visit nearby villages around the city and get patients instead of wasting your time sitting idly in the hospital in waiting for patients. If you do so, I think you will get the patients and the patients won't need to travel to the city for medical services. It will also help you from the trouble of thinking on never ending concerns." With a big smile on his face, he exclaims, "Not a bad idea! Sareeta. I think why I didn't I think of it previously. Your suggestion is absolutely worth welcoming. I will implement it by tomorrow itself."

The next day he goes to the hospital waits for the patients to come. But till noon, no patient comes to please his pocket. He gets up from his chair and leaves the cabin putting the message with the compounder Mahesh that he is on a visit to near by village. He tells him if any one comes register his name call him in the evening till then I will be back. It benefits him not much but at least he gets the chance to see the face of the patients. He continues it for a month or two. During which he meets not more but some patients whose fees solve the problems of his son's fees. After doing it for some months, the doctor gets bored and fed up with this everyday monotonous activity and finally retires to his hopeless chair. Sitting in his thinking hut, he tries to solve the equations of life. For the sake of some amount of rent, he cannot afford to shut down his hospital. The time to pay the rent is about to end. He is sure that his village visits won't do magic. When he finds no way through this, he gets sunk in despair. When he returns home, he shares this problem with his wife, Sareeta. She feels pity for his unfortunate and miserable husband. She takes out her golden bangles and hands over to him. The doctor feels ashamed of himself and says "What are you doing? Stop it. I won't take it. It makes me look down." Supporting him Sareeta says, "Real happiness does not come from wearing ornaments. It comes from happy minds and hearts. If they are not happy, no ornaments can make them happy. Why do we wear ornaments not for look but it is a kind of investment which can help in the period of hard times." He reluctantly takes them and sells them out and pays the rent of the building and continues his profession with new spirit and enthusiasm. It hurts him a lot but with a heavy heart he takes the golden bangles of Sareeta and sells them out to the local goldsmith and thus manages the money to pay the pending rent of the owner. This day is the worst day in his life as it has raised a question mark on his ability as an earning husband. It is the noon's time; he is engaging himself with a newspaper, all of a sudden, his eyes catch news of a business conference for the doctors in Mumbai. He gets troubled with the concluding line of the news that the conference attending doctors won't be given accommodation. It troubles him but soon he comes out of it and determines to attend it.

He comes home and tells his wife Sareeta that he is going to Mumbai tomorrow morning to attend a business conference for the doctors. He reaches to Mumbai and takes a room in a lodge located in a slum area as it is cheap and close from the conference venue. He attends the meeting gets frustrated at ideas of the business shared and discussed in the conference as the ideas are not effective enough to end his concerns. He turns unhappy not over attending meeting but spending on such a useless meeting. He returns to the lodge at about 6: 0opm. After getting fresh, he retires on the bed watching programs on the television. Unknowingly, he keeps the door of his room open which gives him glimpses of the room which is quite in front of his room. He gets shocked to see that a tall but willowy man is sitting in a chair and table before on which he has kept some bags and syringes. When he observes consistently and seriously, he gets further shocked to see that the doctor is receiving a huge amount of money for giving an injection. He thinks that for an injection this much money, he doubts that something is wrong happening there. What surprises him is that when one goes in other is ready to enter. The never ending visitors make him curious to know about the fellow and the magic he does which prospers him. The question which strikes him is how much this doctor would be earning for an injection only.

Seeing the number of notes the fellow earns, Dr. Shrinivasan thinks to meet him and know the secret of his earning. He enters the room and sits on the vacant chair. It is late hour of the evening and the doctor fellow is about to wind up his business. Dr. Shrinivasan occupies the vacant chair for the patient and begins to introduce himself, "Good evening Sir, myself Dr. Shrinivasan from Barahanpur. I have been here to attend the business conference for the doctors. May I know your name please?" Giving him smile, the doctor fellow introduces himself, "I am Dr. Bhatnagar. I am the native of Mumbai. I have been serving as a visiting doctor for last so many years. I have a clinic in Andheri where I rarely go. Most of the times, I am outside serving the patients." He stops in the middle and asks Dr. Shrinivasan about his practice. On receiving this question from Dr. Bhatnagar, the feeling of frustration eclipses his face. But this question on behalf of Dr. Bhatnagar is capable enough to take him in confidence and develops an intimacy with him. Dr. Shrinivasan considering Dr. Bhatnagar to be his well wisher voices his feel of frustration. He says, "I have been practicing in Barahanpur from last five years. But I could not establish myself as a doctor. Very seldom, the patients come to my hospital. This has put me in great financial worries. If it continues for some more time, then it will be very difficult for me to survive and my whole family will be in trouble. Only to get the solution to this corroding concern, I have been here to attend the business conference with the hope that it would offer me a way to survive. But it helped in no way. I am absolutely frustrated with this visit. My worries are really enhancing with every unearned day. I am really helpless and waiting for a savior who would take me out of this situation."

Taking pity on him and to lessen the burden of his worries Dr. Bhatnagar says, "You should not think that this happens to you only. In the initial days of my practice, I had been the victim of all these circumstances. There was a time in my life when it was very difficult for me to manage two times meal since no patient had visited my clinic. But when I found that my medicine practice was not capable to feed me and being unable to do any other business, I decided to live by hook or crook. Luckily I met a doctor friend who taught me how to survive when you fail. He taught me the principle 'If you can't do well then do bad but don't stop living.' Like a true disciple of my savior friend, I have been working on his principle. He taught me that practice which had made him rich. It is the same practice which I have been doing since last several years and see the miracle that I have become sufficiently prosperous person. I have everything now which I had aspired for when began my practice. If you want, I will teach you the way which made me affluent."

Already troubled Dr. Shrinivasan with concerns of survival easily falls prey to his treacherous idea. Dr. Bhatnagar takes a small pouch of powder and mixes it in his injection. He tells him that this is the injection which will give him all that he wants. If he injects it to the patient, the patient will come to him again and pay as much as he demands. Dr. Shrinivasan is mature and wise enough to understand what the powder is about. But pretending to be innocent about the powder, he questions him, "What kind of powder is this? And from where do you get it?" Considering that Dr. Shrinivasan would agree to his saying, he discloses that it is cocaine and in Mumbai you may find a lot of people and doctors doing the business of selling it. There is no harm in doing this business. After all, everyone has a right to lead a happy life. If you want, I can help you. I assure you that this business will take you wherever you wish. It is you to decide the limit. The more you do it, the more you wish to do it as there is no end to one's earning. The more you get the more you wish to earn. This is how the business and life goes on."

The initial response of Dr. Shrinivasan is 'no'. The word 'cocaine' troubles him. But his survival concerns trouble him a lot. Eventually, he tells Dr. Bhatnagar that it is bad but I can't stop living. He tells him, give me a week's time, if I found no fair way to end to my concerns, I will come to you." Dr. Bhatnagar bids him farewell saying, "Take your own time. I am not in hurry. You come to Mumbai whenever you want." Eventually warns to shut his mouth on this issue. Dr. Shrinivasan takes his leave promising him that the he will maintain the secrecy over the meeting and the things discussed. That night goes sleepless as the doctor gets unknowingly engaged in the option of survival offered by his doctor fellow. He returns to Barahanpur.

The next day he goes to his hospital hoping that Mahesh might have received a good number of enquiries from the patients. But his hope turns to be hopeless as Mahesh reports that no one visited the hospital in his absence. His concerns to survive rebegin. The whole day goes in hopeless waiting. Finally he returns home. He takes his silent dinner and retires to his bed. He begins to think over the words of Dr. Bhatnagar, if you can't do good, then do bad but don't stop living. The pendulum of his life vacillates like that of a confused Hamlet of "to be or not to be" in Hamlet and between the two contrary philosophies of Macbeth 'Fair is foul and foul is fair.' After a long troublesome brooding, he comes out of the indecisive world of Hamlet and acts like that of Macbeth. The world of Macbeth provokes him to hurry up and take decision as Macbeth in him doubts that soon Hamlet will overpower him. Dr. Shrinivasan hurriedly picks up his phone at the midnight hour knowing that it would be odd to call Dr. Bhatnagar at this hour of night, to convey his affirmation of his philosophical stand. The next day he leaves Barahanpur for Mumbai. He meets Dr. Bhatnagar in his clinic in Andheri and takes material with assurance to him that he will add his heart and soul in expanding his business. He takes plastic covered cocaine and returns to make his life by spoiling the lives of the others.

He starts practicing it by taking Mahesh in confidence to whom he gives assurance of good hike in his salary. Out of greed for money, Mahesh joins hands with the doctor and manages patients from in and around city. In short period of time, the business of the doctor flourishes. The once time deserted mansion of the hospital turns to be crowdy. Both are happy with never ending entries and exits of the patients coming from various parts of the cities and other villages as well. The doctor's strong conviction in Macbethan philosophy makes his fortune smile upon him. In short span of time Dr. Shrinivasan grows affluent making his compounder Mahesh as well. Dr. Shrinivasan and his loyal compounder Mahesh carry this evil practice for years. Alluring the youths and throwing them into an intoxicating world of cocaine. Day by day the number of addicted youths and people increase and almost half of Barahanpur gets cocaine addicted. Almost half of the population of Barahanpur, from teen agers to the old people, all become his customers. Dr. Shrinivasan, the man who once could not afford to pay for petrol of his bike now comes to his hospital in a new car every day. He purchases the building of his hospital from his owner paying him the desired amount. He renovates the building making it bigger and taller than other doctors. This growth in short span in life raises the eye brows of the surrounding doctors. Most of them come to see him, appreciate his success and to know how he has done it. But Shrinivasan is cunning and practical enough to understand if he tells them, very soon he will be behind the bar so he philosophically answers them only true faith in hard work made him successful. Thus he takes all possible precautions that none should get wind of what he is doing.

After renovating his hospital, he reconstructs his house and turns it into a new bungalow. His wife is excited but truly worried at heart over the sudden change in their lives. She suspects that her husband might have involved in some malpractice as no sincere and honest means give such riches in so short time. Once she doubts her husband. She questions him, "Shrinivasan, don't you think that your progress is miracle as you have climbed the ladder of success so quickly? Look back at those years when you honestly did your service and waited for your patients. What happened overnight that patients have started coming to you in crowd. I doubt that you are doing some magic. Is it not a black magic?" Realizing that his wife is suspecting his sudden advancement, he tries to suppress his wife with somewhat angry tone, "I think you are growing doubtful about me. But see I am doing nothing doubtful. I am just honestly performing my practice and rest is the part of the fortune. If possible hence forth stop doubting and taking interest in what I do and what I don't." She gets silenced with these words and realizes that now he does not like poking nose in his business. But she gets sure that he is doing something wrong.

Once it happens that he goes to Mumbai to bring cocaine. He takes huge stock of cocaine from Dr. Bhatnagar promising him that he would send the amount at the earliest possible. But this time quantity of cocaine is big and its amount is better not to think. He returns home and continues his practice with more vigor. Months passes, but Dr. Shrinivasan does not pay the pending bill of Dr. Bhatnagar which irritates him. Mr. Bhatnagar is constantly in touch with him demanding money. Once they telephonically quarrel like that of a cat and dog. Their contention over pending money concludes with a threat from Dr. Bhatnagar that he will have to pay a huge price, if he does not clear his debts. Dr. Shrinivasan takes it very lightly and there after he never receives the phone of Dr. Bhatnagar mistaking that he would forget him and the money also.

Meanwhile Dr. Bhatnagar sends his agent to Barahanpur to collect the information about Dr. Shrinivasan. The agent brings the information which he desires. Dr. Bhatnagar gets the information that Dr. Shrinivasan has only son, Rohit who is studying in a local college. His evil mind sets on fire. He resends the agent to Barahanpur to catch doctor's son in his trap. The agent comes and hires a flat in Barahanpur and gradually spreads his business. Slowly the college students start coming to his room. Through one of them he succeeds in inviting doctor's son, Rohit on his room where he is forcefully injected. The intoxication of cocaine is such that he becomes the frequent visitor of his room. One day the agent reveals the fact to Rohit that his father has been in this business and works under his leader in Mumbai. Confirming that the doctor's son has been fully trapped in the world of cocaine, the agent leaves Barahanpur. The next day when his body demands intoxication, he leaves the college in the middle and reaches to the agents' room but gets shocked to see that he is not there. On getting enquired, he comes to know that the agent has returned to Mumbai and won't come back. It makes him restless.

Mrs. Shinivasan is keen observer of the movements of her son Rohit and his deteriorating health conditions. She tries to bring it to the notice of her husband but he avoids speaking on this saying that it might be the result of academic pressure. But Mrs. Shrinivasan is quite sure that her son is going astray and maintaining secrecy about his activities. Once, Dr. Shirnivasan is out of his hospital in connection with his work, taking the advantage of his father's absence, Rohit enters the hospital steal packets of pouch and syringe. He hides them under the bed and he consumes them whenever his body demands especially he takes a heavy doses of the intoxicated material at the time of going to bed so that none in the family can get wind of it. Once it happens that Mrs. Shrinvasan is sweeping his room when she finds the empty pouch of cocaine and a syringe which Rohit had forgotten to hide. She gets shocked to see such thing in the bedroom of her son. Her doubt gets confirmed. Without wasting a single moment, she calls her husband home who is in the hospital. Considering the urgency of the visit, Dr. Shrinvasan reaches home. Mrs. Shrinivasan reports him about the things found in the bedroom. She says, "This is the thing I found in the bedroom of Rohit. I had warned you that our son was not looking normal. But you ignored that time. Now see what is happening?" He takes the empty pouch of having some particles of powder and smells it and get it confirmed that it is cocaine. He exclaims, "Oh! My God. It is drugs. Where did he get it? How long has he been consuming. It will put his life in trouble. We are all perished. I need to do something. Where is Rohit? When will he return? Call him wherever he is." Seeing this perished state of her husband, Mrs. Shrinivasan gets broken at heart.

Mrs. Shrinivasan is about to make a phone call to Rohit, suddenly she receives a landline call from her son's college reporting her that their son Rohit is hospitalized and his condition is critical. Hurriedly they reach to the hospital. The examining doctors report the couple that their son's drugs addict and consumption of excessive doses of drugs is responsible for his condition. In a somewhat serious and worried tone he says that his chances of living are very less as the case is gone out of hand. Drugs have totally corroded his body. They don't think that he would recover from this. Asking them to wait for some hours, the doctor goes in the examining hall. The half dead couple anxiously awaits there with the hope that the doctor will come with a smile shortly. Meanwhile the doctor is supporting his almost collapsed wife is willing to make a confession of his clandestine deeds. He is about to open his heart to his wife but suddenly he holds his tongue back as his conscience tells him that this is not the time to make confession otherwise the things will grow worse and it would be very difficult to overpower them. A long unbearable waiting comes to a miserable end as the doctor comes but without smile. Looking at almost half dead couple, the examining doctor conveys the message that they did all that they could to save the life of their son but efforts went in-vain. With heavy tone, the doctor makes the final remark, "I am sorry to say that Rohit is no more."

Mrs. Shrinivasan gets fainted on hearing this cacophonous and heart breaking news. Controlling himself and his uncontrolled wife Dr. Shrinivasan receives the dead body of Rohit and they come back home. The cremation ritual is performed. Grave silence starts ruling their house. Mrs. Shrinivasan has taken her son's death so much to her heart that she grows silent and lies on the bed like that of a corpse. Dr. Shrinivasan wants to talk to her as he has not talked to her for many days but prefers to be silent as he receives no response from her. The compounder Mahesh consistently troubles him with phone calls. One day the doctor receives the phone call from Mahesh who informs him that patients are troubling him a lot and there is never ending line of the patients outside asking for the doctor. Hearing this, he tells him to handle the business for some more days. The condition of Mrs. Shrinivasan grows worse as she has stopped taking food for many days. Dr. Shrinivasan wants to take her to the hospital but her silent negation stops him. One day it is at the time of dusk Mrs. Shrinivasan closes her eyes. Mr. Shrinivasan gets totally collapsed with two consecutive deaths of his dear ones.

The house of the doctor is replete with near and dear ones and enquiring visitors. After some days, when the relatives and the enquiring visitors free the house, he visits the hospital at the time of evening. He tells Mahesh, "Mahesh, my dear you have helped me a lot in all my good and worst times. It is because of your honesty and adherence to me, we could run this illegal business. This business gave you a lot and to me also but it made me pay very heavily. Now I am totally collapsed and cannot afford to run this anymore and spoil the lives of the people as I have realized the value of one's life. Tomorrow I am going to surrender myself to the police for my ill-deeds. I don't want that you should be punished as I think that you don't deserve it because it was I who spoiled your hands. I would like to advise you to leave this place at the earliest before the police reach up to you and live your life away from this city." Mahesh emotionally replies, "Doctor Saheb, you have done a lot for me. I don't want to leave you alone in these worst circumstances but I will follow your advice as I have two kids to be looked after." Mahesh touches the feet of his master and disappears.

Dr. Shivnivasan sits in his vacant chair and takes a final look at the things around. For some moments he enters his past and remembers all those days of struggle and thinks that how happy he was with those days of hardship. Suddenly his mobile rings and he comes back from the flash back world. After answering the call, he gets up from his chair and comes out and takes a last look at the splendid building of the hospital. He feels broken at heart as he cannot bear to see it. With a heavy heart, he shuts down the hospital. He returns home takes out the albums and stares at the family photographs. Seeing his wife and son's photo, he begins to cry loudly. Before going to bed he makes a phone call to nearby police station and confesses his deeds. After sometimes, the police van reaches at the bungalow of the doctor giving cacophonous and ominous sound with the hope that Dr. Shrinivasan would be waiting for them.

When they reach there they find that the main door of the bungalow is open. They enter the bungalow but find none there. Then they move towards the bedroom of Dr. Shrinivasan and finds that it is locked from inside. They call him by his name but no response comes from inside. They suspect of happening of some ominous thing and eventually they break the door and enter the bedroom and get shocked to see that Dr. Shrinivasan has committed suicide by cutting the blood vein of his left hand. The police find a piece of paper kept on the table which speaks like this. "As one sows, so one reaps. I sowed the seeds of poison in the society and the same seeds poisoned me and my family in return. I had become mad in the race of earning money and while doing so I had forgotten that I had been finishing myself. I paid very heavily for what I did. I always thought of myself and my family and never society figured in my life. I was growing at the cost of the others. The patients whom I injected suffered a lot and it is time for me to do penance for what I have done. The deaths of my innocent wife and son have taught me what is worth of one's life. I have preferred this way of confession of my sins to save the life all those who would be trapped by another Dr. Shrinivasan like me and Dr. Bhatnagar. On the back side of the paper the police find the name of Dr. Bhatnagar and other doctors in and around Mumbai involved in this malpractice of abolishing the race of humanity.

Horoscopes

After a long interval of years, the crying sound of a newly born baby shakes the decaying walls and ever leaking teens of a hut on the farm outside the town of Radha Nagari. The baby makes such a loud cry that he is not happy to be here as if he knows what would be his lot here in this Tajmahal of poverty. It is the hut of a couple Shridhar and Janaki who work as farm labor on the farm of a landlord in the town of Radha Nagari. It is this landlord who makes this hut for his farm labor. Poverty has been their greatest legacy which they inherit from their destitute ancestors. They were so happy with their profession as a labor that a thought of having home of their own or having an acre of land could not touch their destitute mind. Earlier generations of Shridhar spent their lives in utter poverty accepting the predictions of their destiny. Their lives spent in shading sweat on the farms of the rich landlords and never had a word of thought how their successors would survive.

Shridhar's father too was a sincere and an honest farm labor whose entire life spent in feeding a huge family of three daughters and one son, Shridhar. One can understand how difficult it would be for a labor to survive such a huge family with his meager income. Like his ancestors, Shridhar's father never thought of going out of tradition which pleased them with pain and suffering. He always thought that he was born to be a labor feeling satisfied on spending sweat on the others' farm enriching the rich landlord. Whatever he had earned spent on the marriages of his three daughters leaving a great heritage of poverty to his only and lonely son Shridhar. Shridhar accepts his lot and carries the heritage of poverty with no aspiration to come out of it. The ancestors of Shridhar migrated from one place to the other in search of their livelihood and eventually settled down in Radha Nagari. Janaki too belonged to a labor's family and have suffered the blows of the poverty. When her marriage had fixed, her father had borrowed some loan which he could not repay till the last breath of his life and died unpaid. So poverty is not new to her and being habitual she becomes quite fit into poverty affected family of Shridhar.

The cry of the newly born baby son brings happiness and hope for the family at the same time enhances the financial worries caused due to his nourishment. The family works day and night for their darling son to whom they name Yashwant with a pure expectation that their son would wipe out their disgrace of poverty and lead a family to the world of affluence. The name Yashwant stands for the person who enjoys success in his life. The family has great hope from their only son and builds castle in the air that their son would grow and bring them good days which their ancestors had never seen for generations.

Once Janaki becomes desirous to know the destiny of her son so hopefully she goes to a well known horoscope maker in Radha Nagari. He studies the stars of Yashwant and makes a destitute horoscope in the sense it shows nothing but poverty for her son. He hands over the horoscope to Janaki saying in nervous tone that the son is unlucky and his stars say that he will spend his whole life in utter poverty. On hearing this, Janaki feels sad and broken at heart and thinks that how long this curse of poverty would hamper their lives. Tears begin to flow from her eyes and dismay eclipses the hopeful smile on her face with which she comes to the horoscope maker. On seeing watery eyes and heart killing consternation on her furrowed face, the horoscope maker asks her what makes her sad. She tells him as if she is opening the horoscopes of her ancestors that how her ancestors had been a great destitute who left nothing but great heritage of poverty for them and what worries her is that the unfavorable stars' curse would make her son suffer. She begs him to do anything but the change this horoscope to safeguard her son from the evil eyes of the destiny. Initially the horoscope maker expresses his inability to change it as it is the words of destiny and no one can do it. Janaki's concern grows and she begins to wail loudly. Seeing her frustration, the horoscope maker gets moved at heart and bends before the suffering of Janaki.

She continues her begging tone to change the destiny of her destitute son and suggesting him let it be a fake one. She controlling her wailing and covering her grief boldly convinces him to make such a fake horoscope which would project her son to be a prosperous and successful. Taking pity on her and the pain which she has suffered, for the first time in his life time, the horoscope maker makes fraud with his own profession and hands over a fake horoscope as she wished. She thanks him and returns to her hut with utter frustration. She does not disclose it to her husband with the fear that he may get nervous and feel frustrated. Bringing an artificial smile on her face she tells Shridhar that Horoscope maker has predicted a bright future for their darling son Yashwant. It gives him happiness and new hope to carry on the legacy of the ancestors' poverty. She hands over the fake horoscope to Shridhar and requests him to keep it safe. She keeps the original destitute horoscope in her old ancestral iron box locks it and pushes it under the cot.

Years pass, Yashwant grows and with that enhances the worries of his parents. They decide to educate their son and get him admitted in one of the schools in Radha Nagari. Yashwant good at studies overcomes the exams after exams and joins the year of Matriculation. The family is very happy with his achievements and feels fully confident that their son would definitely break the tradition of ancestors. This hope becomes the strength of the family and means of survival. Once it rains cat and dog in Radha Nagari. Thundering sound and eyes hurting lightening shakes the placid life of the people in the town. To protect from heavy rain, Shridhar takes shelter under a huge mango tree. Suddenly a noisy serpent like wave of lightening falls on Shridhar and steals away his life.

It is a great setback for the family. Janaki falls ill and gets confined in the bed. Yashwant stops going to school and spends whole time looking after ailing mother. Once again cruel destiny whips the family very mercilessly. This year Yashwant has to crack his Matriculation's examination. But illness of his mother grows day by day rarely giving him time to look at the academics. With the help of the landlord he manages a doctor from other city but Janaki has taken her husband's death to heart that she slowly stops responding to the medicine of the doctor. Yashwant does nothing but helplessly watches his dying mother. One day it is at the time of dusk, Janaki takes her last breath and departs from this world leaving her a legacy of poverty behind for her son. Yashwant completely broken at heart by the series of the severe jolts of destiny any how performs the ritual of funeral.

A few days later, when he is lying on the wooden cot thinking about his dear departed mother, thinks to find the memories of his mother. He knows that there is an iron box which she used to open and close it for number of times. He is sure that he may find some things of his mother which will please him. He unlocks the iron box and finds some folded saris and a knot of a cloth which he opens and finds some coins and rolled notes. At the bottom of the iron box, he finds some spiritual books. He picks one of them and just turns pages one after the other and suddenly his eyes catch a folded piece of paper. Curiously, he unfolds it and finds that it is his horoscope. He seriously looks at it and gets sunk in despair because the content in it steals his hope and courage. It is written in it that there are no chances of good fortune for the newly born baby. His whole life will go in poverty. The prediction affects his psyche. It changes the very course of his action. He loses his interest and becomes absolute hopeless. He develops such an attitude which suits to the prediction of the horoscope.

There is draught like situation in Radha Nagari as there is no rain for two years and farms turn out to be desert. One day the landlord asks Yashwant to find a job somewhere else because he cannot afford to keep him on the farm as it stopped producing. It hurts him a lot. He takes a small room on rent in Radha Nagari. Troubled routine life weakens him physically as well as mentally too. Soon he joins the company of the negative people and goes astray. He gets involved in evil activities and becomes a thorough drunkard. He loses all hopes to make future as he strongly believes in the prediction of destiny.

To manage his expenses, he begins to work in a tea stall. Whole day he works at this tea stall and as the darkness falls, he begins his evil activities. He gets involved in playing cards and gambling and loses all that he earns from the tea stall. One day he returns to his room in a drunken state. While lying on his cot an old, dull and somewhat dirty cloth bag hanging at the wooden hook arrests his attention and beacons him to find the treasure of inspiration hidden in the darkness within the bag. This bag has never been an allurement for Yashwant and has never felt needy to open it and see what is there in. Suddenly, he begins to feel an allurement for it as if it seems to him to be a guiding light in his dark period. He gets up from his wooden cot and takes it down. He curiously opens it with a feeling and eagerness to see what treasure has been hidden in this bag by his father. He feels frustrated on finding that there are nothing but a wallet like leather bag and some notebooks. Feeling unattached for the books he keeps them aside and eagerly opens the chain of the wallet to see how much treasure has been left for him by his father. He feels little pleased to see some hundred rupees notes and some coins. Then he slowly opens the zipped chain of an inner pocket. He opens the chain and finds a well folded piece of a paper. Softly and slowly he reaches into the inner world of the folded paper. He gets shocked to see a one more horoscope of his name. He gets disturbed with this but with blended feeling of fear and astonishment, he starts reading the prediction. He feels in seventh heaven to read the prediction that he would be very illustrious and successful business man. He takes it to be true and blames the horoscope maker who made the first one and abuses him for wrong prediction which gives him an unbearable trauma. At a particular moment a thought comes to his mind to meet the horoscope maker and abuse him but he withdraws from the thought with fear that he may predict something else for him.

He fully trusts in this prediction and comes out of an evil spell of hypnotized world of negativism. He gives up his old approach as a snake gives up his old and decayed skin which is supposed to be the new birth of the snake. He mentally prepares to eclipse his black history and writes a new history of success and hope. He thinks and acts on the prediction of the second horoscope. One day while taking some vegetables in the bazaar day of Radha-Nagari, he happens to meet an old woman selling pickles. He stops there looking at the hopeful and furrowed face of the old woman. He does not want to commit the sin of saying no to that old lady whose furrowed face tells him the history of her suffering. Taking pity on her and her struggle to survive in this old age with the meager income, Yashwant takes out some coins and hands over to the old woman who in return gives him some pickles.

After exchanging happy smile with each other, Yashwant returns home. He sits for lunch and tastes the pickles and finds that it to be very tasty. The taste of pickles arouses in him a desire to learn the art of making pickles. The next bazaar day, he intentionally meets the old lady and honestly appreciates her skill of making pickles and expresses a heartfelt desire to learn the art of making pickles. The old lady unobjectionably gets ready and takes him her home. As Yashwant has no other commitments, he goes and stays with woman for next couple of months. He also accompanies her to the bazaar on the bazaar day. She finds him to be a helping hand and treats him to be like her own son. Yashwant too feels that he has regained his loving mother Janaki in the form of this old lady. They are bound together in the threads of emotions. In short span of time, Yashwant acquires the skill of making variety of tasty pickles and spices which fixed his future. After some days, the old woman dies telling him the way to be rich. As she has none of her blood relation, Yashwant acts as a son and performs all the responsibilities of death and ritual that comes after.

Optimistic and industrious Yashwant starts his independent business of pickles. Now he takes the place of old woman in bazzar. On every bazzar day in Radha Nagari, he sits there selling and loudly appealing and requesting the customers for having pickles. Within a few days, his tasty pickles and spices become the favorite taste of the people of Radha Nagari and nearby places. His business flourishes with that his fame as a pickle maker too. He earns enough and an ambitious thought of expanding his business blooms in his mind. He takes a shop on rent where he keeps pickles for sale. As the demand grows, he starts sending packed pickles and spices to the people. The popularity of the taste of products starts spreading all over the state which gives him a state level recognition. But he has not stopped going to the bazzar from where he flew like a Phoenix in the endless world of enterprise. The business grows day by day enhancing Yaswant's responsibilities. To lighten the burden of his responsibilities he recruits sufficient labor. When it is not possible to go to bazzar for selling pickles, he sends one of his boys to do the work, thus he continues his tradition.

Considering the growing demands for his products, he starts his industries and spending a lot on the machinery and labor. In short span of time he starts expanding the roots of his business over the state. He starts a big project at Rahda Nagari which gives employment to the localities which makes him very popular. He succeeds in earning a lot of respect in the town. There is no field which is free from his influence. His word has a great respect in Radha Nagari as he has been an impartial and well-wisher of the town. He finances many projects useful for the people, finances various NGOs and finances to social development oriented activities. Thus he emerges as a social reformer. He takes a lot of pain to be success on both the fronts. His business magically grows day by day making him the most influential businessman in the state. He emerges as a businessman who keeps the capability to influence the state economy.

To inculcate the virtue of enterprise, industry and passion for success, the state government introduces a lesson on the life of Yashwant in the state's curriculum of Matriculation. It also confers on him the most coveted honor of 'Udyogratna'. The government gets overwhelmed by his humanitarian approach and his devoted service to the society and honors him with its greatest honor. The media always hungry for breaking news becomes eager to cover the life stories and achievements of Yashwant. In an interview on television, the Journalist questions Yashwant, "How does he succeed?" He humorously answers, "It is all the magic of double horoscopes and nothing else."

After this interview, he returns home. When he is lying on his bed, he goes back into the charming magical world of horoscopes and feels desired to see the person who played the game on him. He gathers the information that there is only one family in entire Radha Nagari which makes horoscopes. On the next day he reaches to the house with two horoscopes to know whether they have made it. The son of the old horoscope maker is there. Seeing the horoscopes he discloses that it is his father who made it. On enquiring, Yashwant comes to know that the old horoscope maker is still alive and has retired from this service. He expresses his willingness to see the old gentleman.

Being aware of the status and recognition of Yashwant, the son of the horoscope maker respectfully takes him in the room where the old gentleman is resting. On seeing Yashwant, the old horoscope maker gets up to receive him. Yashwant opens the pages of past history and tells him that long back his mother had made two horoscopes and does not forget to add that both the horoscopes are after his name and questions with great curiosity and surprise. "How can a person have two horoscopes? What is the mystery behind it?" The very reference of two horoscopes reminds him the wailing sound of Janaki and her consistent begging. He narrates the whole story behind it. He discloses to Yashwant that that was the first and the last time in his life when he made two horoscopes of the same person and it was on the request of that destitute mother who never wanted her son to be a destitute like her ancestors. He unfolds the mystery behind it saying that the first horoscope predicts that Yashwant would be a destitute is true and that is reality and the second is false one and was made on the request of his mother. Then Yashwant questions him how his prediction proved to be false one and he became according to what has been written in the second one? On this, the old gentleman unfolds the basic truth of his business. He says making horoscopes is sheer business for him and for all those who do it. They have some fundamental knowledge on which they make horoscopes. They are not extraordinary men or some divine powers to peep into the future of a person and make prediction accordingly. They are common men of flesh and blood and if they had such power in them, there would not have any difference between them and the creator. The people who come to them for horoscopes do not understand it and believe that whatever they put in the horoscope is true. If written well they become happy and if written badly they get disappointed and start begging either to change it or to give remedies to overcome it. It is not their fault that they do it as it's the matter of their bread and butter. He says very candidly, it is up to the people to decide whether to accept it or to discard it. But the people who don't dare to do it get influenced by the prediction in the horoscope and fix the course of action.

Commenting on the false prediction of Yashwant which comes true, the old gentleman says, "Yashwant, it is not the horoscope that changed and made him great success. But it is right approach and hard work at the right time made him what he is today. He tells him and advises that there is nothing like a horoscope and humorously questions him who are they to make his future? Thanking old horoscope maker, Yashwant comes out of the house. Staring at the two horoscopes, he smiles and tears them into pieces and throws them into nearby drainage.

Red Inspiration

It is the morning time. A person is engaged in reading a newspaper in his placid cabin. It is the cabin in a hospital and the person reading a news paper is the world famous personality Dr. Raghunathan. He is world famous in the sense that his charm of magical abilities in the profession of medicines has spread all over the world. He is heart surgeon and has been responsible for giving life to many heart patients worldwide. His hospital is always replete with the patients from all corners of the nation and widely from the distant corners of the world. Sometimes he is invited to U.S.A. and United Kingdom for performing very delicate and critical heart surgeries. When a patient comes to know that he will be operated by Dr. Raghunathan, he becomes sure that it will be a success as such is the name, fame and recognition of Dr. Raghunathan. Patients feel half cured with the very presence of Dr. Raghunathan. He has performed ample heart surgeries and never failure could dare to spoil his hands. Dr. Raghunathan and success has become popular equation. His surgery skills make him one of the richest people in Bangalore. For the accommodation of a large number of patients, he has built a huge, capacious and splendid hospital in one of the lanes of Bangalore.

Everyday there is never ending rush of the patients. But today the hospital seems to be a little crowdy as most of the heart patients have been relived with successful heart surgeries. Dr. Raghunathan is so busy that he rarely gets time to throw a look at the newspaper. It is on one of such mornings, he finds some leisure which he uses for casting a look at the newspaper. Suddenly a young and beautiful receptionist disturbs the placidity of the cabin and brings Dr. Raghunathan back from the world of newspaper. She comes with the message that a couple has been waiting to see him. The doctor asks her to send them in. The couple has come with a huge bouquet. Dr. Raghunathan gratefully receives the bouquet of flowers and welcomes them. The husband uncovers the intention of their coming saying that they have come here to express their sincerest gratitude for giving a new life to the couple. The husband of the woman says that it is because of his magical hands, he could live and see this beautiful world otherwise he had lost his hopes. Dr. Raghunathan does not remember the couple as he has performed so many surgeries in India and abroad and so it is not so easy to remember whom he met where and when? Doctor thanks them and offers a cup of tea. After having tea and finishing their talk, the couple disperses.

Immediately after the departure of the couple, there comes a rich, well dressed woman. It's Mrs. Janaki Raghunathan, the wife of the doctor. She too does her medicine practice in the same hospital. Mrs. Janaki Raghunathan is Gynecologist. She too is responsible for many successful natural deliveries and caesarian of women. Her medicinal powers have enabled many barren women to conceive. She has successfully conducted the experiment of test tube baby program in her hospital and given women the pleasure of womanhood which cannot be complete without attaining the ability to be a mother. She has given children to many women and heirs to many childless but affluent families.

Unfortunate thing about this couple is that they are personally troubled by a grave concern. It is the inability of Mrs. Janaki Raghunathan to conceive. They are married for eight years yet Mrs. Janaki Raghunathan is still going through the state of childlessness. The doctor couple has taken the treatment and advice of widely acknowledged and most successful doctors in the field of gynecology in and out of India. But nothing could bring to her the happiness of being a mother. The concern corrodes the family and steals the cheerfulness from their life. Being doctors, they don't believe in magic of spiritual powers. Even if they want to believe, their rational conscience won't let them do it. This may be the reason that they never visit any temple nor they consult with any 'Baba' who can give them a 'mantra' to overcome the concern of infertility.

Once, grandmother of Mrs. Janaki Raghunathan comes to stay with them. She has deliberately come to stay with them so that she can share a few words of wisdom with the troubled couple. The great grand lady suggests that there is a very popular temple of goddess in a village at a distance of 25 kilometers away from Bangalore and it is believed and it is a deeply rooted conviction among the people that if an infertile woman worships this Goddess, the barren woman is blessed with the child and this has been proved to be true number of times. She wants that the couple should visit the temple of Goddess and try to gain her blessing. Initially, the couple is not ready to do it, but on consistent requesting approach of their grandmother, they finally decide to visit that magical place.

On one fine and fresh morning, the couple goes to the temple and performs necessary rituals and returns home. A few months after the visit to the temple, magically Mrs. Janaki becomes pregnant bringing never ending fountains and showers of cheerfulness to the troubled and frustrated Dr. Raghunathan. The jubilant couple sends the note of gratitude to the grandmother giving credit of pregnancy to her and now their Goddess who has removed the darkness of despair from their lives. The couple wholeheartedly admits that it is the blessing of the goddess in the temple. The day of delivery comes, after a lot of pains; Mrs. Janaki gives birth to male child which takes the couple above the Moon. The news of birth of male child in Doctor's family spreads like fragrance all over. Cured patients, doctors, colleagues and his social political acquaintances shower on the couple the flowers of congratulations. Many come to congratulate and to see them personally to be the part of and witness of this most memorable event in the life of the doctor couple. Naming ceremony of the baby is arranged. Baby boy is named "Palak". People from all fields give their presence on this occasion.

Once, the couple visits the temple to express their feeling of gratitude and get blessings of the goddess. Dr. Raghunathan observes that the temple is quite small and in -capacious and want of facilities and causes lot of inconveniences to the devotees. Suddenly an idea comes in his mind to do some work of happiness for the temple as a part of his feeling of gratitude. After coming from the temple, Dr. Raghunathan shares his plan to expand and reconstruct the temple with his wife. Dr. Janaki who too gets overwhelmed by this idea. They call their architect friend and put the plan before him. He agrees and makes wonderful outline of the proposed temple which is finally approved. As it is a huge plan it takes years for completion. Dr. Raghunathan finding time from his busy schedule visits the construction site of the temple.

Once, a poor widow comes with her ailing son in the hospital. She tells the Doctor that the son has been suffering from heart problem since he was eight years old. But due to poor financial condition and as there is no one to support her; she unwillingly avoided to take him to the doctor. But the ailing condition of her son has reached its serious stage and hearing Doctor's name, she has come here. She begs the doctor to save her son. The doctor takes the boy in the operation theater examines him and comes to the conclusion that the heart of the baby needs to be operated. Doctor tells her that the son's heart problem which can be cured by an operation which would charge her one lakh rupees. On hearing the huge amount, the poor widow feels to be fainted doctor controls and offers her a glass of water so that she would feel comfortable. She tells the doctor that she cannot afford to spend such a huge amount and hurriedly she takes her son back. The tears begin to come out of the eyes of the woman. Doctor asks her, "What is the reason of your tears?" To this she replies that she lost her husband a few years back. He was a great drunkard. He sold all that he had to quench his thirst for wine and keeping us hungry permanently. When he died, she did not have money to perform his cremation ritual. Some elderly gentle men helped her and paid some money so that she could perform the funeral rituals. He went leaving her to die with this dying son. After her husband's death, she began to work as maid servant earning the money which would give her two times food for her little family. She says to Doctor that she wants to take her son back as she cannot afford the expenses and ironically says let him die, she does not care for it at least it would free her permanently from the routine concern.

Doctor gets moved by the record of the suffering of woman's life. Without wasting a moment, he prepares for the operation. After an hour, Doctor comes out of the operation theatre gives a smile of success to the anxious poor widow outside. He calls her in and tells her that operation is successful and the boy is alright now. Without taking a single rupee, Doctor discharges the boy. Mother does not have words to say thanks. Giving a weeping smile to Doctor, she takes the son and goes away. Doctor feels happy for what he has done. He thinks that this is profession in real sense. But on the very next moment, he feels troubled over the discreet judgment of God. How that God gives heirs to the family cursed with poverty and makes affluent family as a heirless?

The renovation work of the temple continues for years. Doctor couple is busy in profession saving the lives of the people on one side and ceaselessly taking care of growing son Palak who joins his fifth standard on other side. The renovation work of the temple ends. Doctor couple organizes a grand function in the temple. There comes the crowd of the people to attend the function. All enjoy meal arranged by the doctor couple and the trustees of the temple. Doctor couple and their son Palak take meal and come back home at the time of evening. That day, they don't prepare dinner and go to bed. The next day morning Palak does not get up at his usual time. The anxious Dr. Janaki tries to wake him up but Palak does not respond. He has become completely energy-less and unable to lift himself. Dr. Janaki gets shocked by this sudden physical change occurred in her son overnight. Dr. Raghunathan comes in the chamber of Palak examines his body and gives him primary aids.

Dr. Raghunathan wants Palak to get shifted in his hospital but Palak refuses to do it. The condition of Palak becomes worse day by day. He stops taking food rarely giving positive response to fruits juice. Doctor couple suffers a lot of trauma due to this unexpected miserable plight of their loving son. Dr. Raghunathan uses all his medical expertise to cure this hidden and un-curable disease. He calls his colleagues who are well known doctors to make diagnosis of Palak's ailment but their medicines too do no magic. With the degrading condition of Palak, grows the concern of the family too. They leave no stone unturned to provide all possible treatment to Palak so that he would recover his illness and once again join their active life smiling and pleasing all with his mesmerizing look.

Dr. Raghunathan calls his overseas doctor friends to cure his son. They too come but their hands fail to bring about the desired improvement in the degrading health of Palak. Palak almost feels paralyzed lying on his bed like a corpse staring lifelessly at the things around. All the beautiful things stop appealing him now. The thing of beauty has become grief forever. The part of his body below the neck has become movement less. Only the beating of the heart is observed. The face has become pale and a little life his left in the eyes with which he enjoys the things around. When the visitors come to see him, they stand still and wait that Palak would give them smile but they return disappointedly. Doctor couple feels half dead over the ceaselessly degrading condition of their son. For the first time, they feel themselves utterly failed and helpless and blame themselves for not curing their son.

Once, the old mother of Dr. Janaki Raghunathan visits Palak and suggests them to perform pooja at the temple of Goddess and beg for the life of Palak. As a last chance, the couple performs pooja with the hope that the blessing of the goddess would revive almost dead Palak. But this time, the blessing of the goddess too shows no magic. The hopeless doctor couple does nothing but helplessly watching and shading tears on the slowly dying life of Palak. Once, a distant relative of doctor's family comes to enquire of Palak's health. Before leaving the chamber, he puts a beautiful rose in an empty glass on the table. The rose is beautiful and enchanting that Palak too takes deliberate note of the presence of it. It seems to him that the flower has come here as an agent of god and would make him happy in his last days. Now, Palak stops staring at other artifacts surrounding him as they seem to be dull and unpleasant and devotes his staring in the service of the beautiful rose. Palak looks at it as if the standing rose in the glass is communicating with him and telling him the truths and mysteries of human life.

The passing time gradually steals the beauty of the rose and turns it into an ugly object. He looks dry and lifeless. It hurts little Palak and makes him feel more dead. The rose grows dryer and dryer making the base of the flower to let loose its hold on the petals. Palak is too much disturbed with it. He feels that the every drying petal of rose wants to tell him something. He grows very much eager in his staring and watches very keenly and minutely the movements taking place within the flower. Palak's staring is confined to the dying rose only. The doctor couple has stopped going to the hospital. When they sit at the dining table to have food, the empty chair of Palak sinks them in despair. Number of times it happens that they leave eating food in the middle and return to the Palak's chamber to spend time with their ever hungry Palak. They do nothing but continuously sitting beside Palak. They feel broken at hurt and feel almost collapsed as if they have become quite sure that their future support is gradually losing its root and may collapse at any moment.

Palak's interest in the dying flower grows day by day. The base of the rose makes its grip looser and makes them free one by one. Palak is staring at the flower as if he has connected himself with the rose totally forgetting and ignoring the presence of the human beings around him. It is the time of dusk, the first petal of the rose falls but before falling it seems that the petal teaches him the lesson that life is mortal. Everyone has his day when he has to attend a divine call from heaven. It says to him the fools are those who are afraid of death. It seems to him that it is questioning to him why people forget that it is the death that ends all the miseries of human life. Death is as beautiful as life and if they believe it to be ugly then equally ugly is the life too. So, wisdom lies not in escaping from the death but accepting it. There is no sense in mourning over death. It is not the end but a fresh beginning with new body and new life. The reality expressed by the dropping petal contributes to the wisdom of Palak and makes him feel somewhat relaxed inwardly. With each passing day, there falls the petal of the rose. Once time beautiful rose looks ugly and resembles to the man having no limbs. The last petal of the rose is counting its last breath. Its time is yet to come. Day by day it bends down as if it is paying its last respect to his great lover. It is about to fall. Palak is fully engrossed in staring at the bending petal of the almost dead rose. It is at the last stroke of the mid night hour, the petal gets ready for its fall. Palak is about to shade tears for the departing petal, suddenly it seems to him the bending petal has deliberately bent forward to tell him one of the greatest thought of wisdom of human existence. He totally submits himself to the last petal. The falling petal looks at Palak and gives him the last but beautiful smile and empowers and encourages him with its last message of philosophy of human existence.

The petal says to Palak that birth and death is the greatest gift of God. Birth gives a unique chance to everyone to see this beautiful world and enjoy the every thing of beauty around him. Death gives him freedom from the miseries of the life. The petal further adds that behind the birth of every life, there is a purpose. God sends everyone on this earth with a destined purpose. Unless, that purpose is served, the divinity does not call him back. The petal says to Palak that he is especial child of the destiny and a great work is expected from him. The purpose of his life is yet to be served and till then death won't dare to touch him. It ignites a hope to live in the heart of Palak. Suddenly, the last petal falls down muttering last word "Get up Palak! You are to live to do something great."

The next morning, Palak gets up early in the morning and finds that his parents are sleeping down stairs. He comes out calmly; there is a beautiful garden in the front yard of the bungalow. Palak feels extremely delighted to see a beautiful rose bloomed in the garden. It seems to him that the departed flower has come back to see him and wish him a very happy new life. Palak smiles at the flower and kissing it; he moves towards another flower and gets engrossed in watching it.

Doctor couple gets shocked to see that Palak is not there on the bed. They start searching him here and there but they don't find him in the house. Dr. Raghunathan comes out to take a look around the house and gets shocked and felt extremely pleased to see Palak engrossed in gazing at the periwinkle flower in the garden. Dr. Janaki Raghunathan too comes out hurriedly and gets surprised to see her loving son who was confined in the bed till yesterday is loitering in the garden. Doctor couple surprisingly looks at each other and questions how is it possible? Is it not a miracle? Whatever it may be good thing is that they have got their son back. It is a day of jubilation for the entire family.

The whole family celebrates this miracle by arranging a grand feast for their acquaintances and relatives. The house is overcrowded to congratulate the whole family over this extra-ordinary and miraculous achievement. The doctor couple feels in the seventh heaven with the miraculous recovery of Palak. That night, her son couple chats for long time and sleeps with a hope that they would be able to recover the secret behind their son's sudden recovery.

Years pass, the doctor couple has grown sufficiently old now. They want that their son to be a doctor like them and should shoulder the responsibility of their huge hospital. But they soon realize that their son is not interested in their profession and his interest is in plants especially he is attracted towards flowers. After completing his twelfth with science with good marks, he expresses his desire to be a master in science and especially in botany. He says that he has a great attraction for plants and he would like to study flowers, if he gets a chance. Being a lonely son and loving, the doctor couple prefers to keep their own will aside and give their full preference to their son's will. Palak completes his M.Sc. in Botany. One day, he expresses his desire to undertake a research activity in his subjects. The family agrees with his decision. He joins university as a research scholar, he does experiments with flowers. His curiosity is that he wants to know what is that ingredient or a chemical which keeps the petals intact and fresh all the time and why not after their being plucked. It is his will that petals should be as fresh and colorful as they were before they were plucked and wants that the beautiful flower should meet his end with all its petals intact and lively as they were. Through his years' experimentations and hard work, he succeeds in discovering liquid, if it is injected in the base of the rose, the petals remain intact and fresh even after plucking. He does this experiment on the flowers in his garden. He takes an un-injected and injected rose plant. He plucks them and keeps them in his bed room. After some days, he finds that the petals of an un-injected rose have fallen down and the petals of the injected one remain intact and fresh as if it has just been plucked. He goes closer to the injected flower. It seems to him that the flower is a distant relative of that old one which gave him the hope to live, smiles at him and says that 'Thank you for beautifying my death."

Soon he starts injecting the vaccine in all the flowers plants and he finds the same result in all the flowers. Flowers are happy that they are saved from the sufferings of the old age and being ugly. The news of research success spreads like a wild fire and showering on him the praise and honors. The matter of pride is that the Nobel Prize for scientific discovery is declared to Palak's research accomplishment.

One day curious father asks Palak about his interest in flowers. To this, Palak replies very emotionally and philosophically. He says that he is indebted to that rose flower which gave him a new hope and new life. He tells his father that the rose taught him the greatest lesson of life that life comes with a purpose. It made him realize the purpose of life ignited and empowered him to get up and begin a new life with a sole aim to serve the purpose of his life. He emotionally adds that what troubled him about the flower is the way the beautiful rose flower died. At first the beautiful rose flower turned ugly and slowly its delicate petals started falling down. There is no doubt that life is beautiful then why not the 'Death' and there would be nothing unjust, if the death becomes beautiful. When the petals of the flower were separating and falling down, it seemed to him that a human being is cut into smaller pieces. It is a death in fragments and looks ugly. Death should be beautiful, fresh and always complete one. Finally, he discloses the intention of his research interest that he wanted to beautify the 'Death' so that every flower would be happy to die.

It is out of his emotional attachment to that red inspiring flower to which he owes as he made him what he is today so he involved himself into the research work on the lives of the flowers.

Dr. Raghunathan gets overwhelmed by the philosophical discourse with his doctor son and gives a pat on his back and proud smile and disperses on his mission.

Penance

Today appears with its specialty on the canvas of the life of a newly trained heart surgeon Dr. Rangrajan. Dr. Rangrajan feels on the top of the air as this day is going to be recorded as the most memorable day in his life history. This day has brought for him a unique opportunity of being a part of a team of heart surgeons who are preparing for heart surgery of a woman. This is going to be a debut performance of Dr. Rangrajan in the domain of heart surgeries. He is hoping with confidence that he would heartily contribute to make it a success. The Parents of Dr. Rangranjan are in great rapture as their son has stood up quite high in their esteem by fulfilling their expectations except one which is left be to be fulfilled that is they want to see the marriage of their only son. The mission of finding a desirable bridegroom is in progress. They are not at all disheartened over not getting desired choice early as they are fully aware of the fact that there is time for everything and they cannot make the knots of marriage as they are already made in the heaven. The mother serves the breakfast and gives a loving call to the doctor. Dr. Rangrajan comes fully prepared and enjoys his breakfast. Dr. Rangrajan looks confident and cheerful. What makes him cheerful is the thought that almighty has offered him the first chance to live for the sake of others. He thinks that there is no other way to serve the society than saving the lives of the others with one's skills. Dr. Rangrajan moves towards his destination with pleasant greetings of 'best of luck' from his loving parents.

It is the late hour of the morning. The conditions in the hospital have taken serious look. There is hustle and bustle everywhere in the hospital especially at the operation theatre. The frequent entries and exits of the nurses into the operation theatre contribute to the swiftness and intensify the importance of the mission to be performed. The voice of someone sitting there in the hospital falls on the ears and its sound says "it is the preparation of the operation to be performed shortly." Suddenly one of the nurses says that all the things are at their places; preparation is almost done and they are waiting for the doctors to come. A beautiful woman nicely dressed makes her entry in the empty space outside the operation theatre. She is accompanied by a person who looks to be of her age and an endearing son may be seven or eight years old. It becomes the first impression of everyone present there that the man accompanying the woman is her husband but when the boy addresses him as uncle, the confusion regarding their relation and identities gets removed. The name of the boy is also revealed through ceaseless shouting of the lady over naughtiness of her son. She shouts little bit angrily "Rohan don't do this. Rohan, don't do that." But Rohan pays no heed to these shouting and enjoys his naughtiness.

A nurse comes and asks the woman to get ready, the doctors are coming shortly. After sometime, the woman is taken into the operation theater and the door of the operation theatre gets locked from inside. Rohan's uncle become serious and the furrows on his face reflect his terrified and gloomy state of mind. But Rohan a happy go lucky boy is engrossed in his playing doing mischief and completely ignorant of the things happening around him. Once, finding time out of his playing, he questions his uncle, "Where is my Mummy? When will she return? What happened to her? Why has she been taken to that room?" To continue him in his naughtiness and hide the things happening to his Mummy, the uncle falsely replies, "She is with the doctor discussing about her problem; have patience as there is nothing worth worrying. She will return soon." On hearing these satisfactory answers, Rohan continues his game of naughtiness. Uncle deliberately entertains his naughtiness as he is sure that if he disturbs him or shouts at him, Rohan may ask for his Mummy and if he fails to produce her, Rohan may take the entire hospital on his head.

There is a pin drop silence in the operation theatre. Words rest in nest of silence and eyes turn garrulous and hands start their dancing performance. All are engrossed in the mission. Dr. Rangrajan is seen engrossed in contributing to the mission. Of and on they exchange smiling eyes with one another conveying the message that operation is going through its several phases of success. All the doctors put an end to the movements of their hands and look at Dr. Rangrajan with great expectations to take his turn and finalize the thing. He begins his turn and nurse passes scissors. Abruptly his hands start shaking with fear and accidently or it may be destined that he cuts the measure vein which supplies blood to the heart and there starts never ending bleeding. Scissors become mischievous and destiny serves its purpose spoiling the lives of the 'both.' Suddenly one of the doctors shouts, "What you did my friend? How can your hands act so foolishly at this important juncture?" They get terrified as their all efforts to stop bleeding go in vain. The doctors and the nurses stare at Dr. Rangrajan with blaming eyes. Dr. Rangranjan cannot have the courage to face these blaming eyes. He gets drowned into flood of sweat looking helplessly and expecting a helping hand at this critical moment of his life. Considering the miserable plight and long future ahead of Dr. Rangrajan, the team of the doctor decides unanimously not to reveal the truth to anyone and all the nurses are strictly warned to keep their tongues on silent mode.

One of the elderly doctors comes out of the operation theatre looking somewhat seriously and worriedly at long and anxiously awaiting man and the little boy hopefully looking at him. Rohan's uncle reads the lines on the furrowed face of the doctor and anticipates happening of something undesirable. But pretending to be positive and optimistic he questions, "What happened doctor? Why are you bowing down as if you have done something undesirable? Is Rohan's mother all right?" Before uncle continues his never ending questions, the doctor stops him and supports him putting his hand on shoulders. He says, "We did all that we could do but our hands could do no miracle. They betrayed us. She is no more." Rohan's uncle sits down and sinks in never ending flood of tears. All the doctors come out of the operation theatre and crowd around the mourning uncle. Seeing Uncle wailing, the confused and now terrified Rohan also starts crying.

Dead body of Rohan's mother is brought out of the operation theatre and hands over to Rohan's uncle. Seeing the dead body of his sister, Rohan's uncle cannot control himself and starts crying. On seeing his uncle crying, Rohan gets further terrified and tries to jump on the stretcher to get up his mother. His wailing sound speaks, "My dear mother! Why are lying like a dead one on this bed? What happened to you? Why this silence for? You talked to me a few minutes ago? Why not now? You said to me you are coming shortly and you have come like this. When will you get up tell na, tell na?" Rohan's questions with a loud wailing continue, seeing the misery of the boy, all there get moved by it. One of the nurses comes forward lifts Rohan and tries to make him calm. Nothing could calm him then finally there comes sleep takes him away from all.

Dr. Rangrajan standing like a culprit with guilty conscience at edge of the group of the doctors sees the condition of the little boy Rohan and sinks in despair. Dr. Rangrajan returns home. The happiness of the morning suddenly disappears leaving room to the mourning of Dr. Rangrajan. His mother asks him, "what happened? Why is your face coloured with a grave silence and you look as if you have committed a heinous crime? Is everything OK? What about the operation? You made it a success?" Without letting her to raise any more questions and trouble his already troubled mind, he betrays with silence and says, "No. I failed." The memory of wailing sound of Rohan awakens his conscience and he starts shouting like an insane one, "I killed her! I am a murderer! I have spoiled two lives! Mummy, what penance is there for such a crime?" Seeing her son totally disturbed holds him tightly and tries to console him saying and encouraging him, "It is destined and who can change her writing?" She advises him to close his eyes to the past and make a new beginning. They sit for dinner together. But mourning sound of Rohan steals his mood and returns to his bedroom with half tasted dinner. Interiors in the bedroom seem to be somewhat gloomy and the soul of the bed room feels suffocated and restless with the presence of dismayed Dr. Rangrajan. It is a sleepless night as the thought of the deed to which Dr. Rangrajan names "A crime" overpowers his sleep and leads him into realm of insomnia for some more days. Dr. Rangrajan is habitual to put off the light in his room before retiring to bed but that night the light enjoys no sleep.

The thought of a crime of killing corrodes him inwardly and rules on his brain for a long time. He stops going to the hospital as he does not want any more crime to be committed at his betraying hands. One day lying on his restless bed and staring at harmless light of the bulb in his bedroom, conscience awakes with the sound of the unstable pendulum. Conscience tells him the way to take a penance for what he has done. It gives him a word of advice and brings back the disappeared peace in his life. Conscience says to encourage the discouraged Dr. Rangrajan, Wake up! Forget whatever happened! It happened as something good is expected to happen by your hands. There is way to wipe out the odor of blood from his hands as he takes it to be a crime? Dr. Rangrajan enters the realm of the conscience and asks her, "How can I get rid of it?" Conscience tells him, "Adopt the boy and learn to live for him." With this consoling and reliving words Conscience disappears to her kingdom. Dr. Rangrajan gets up from the bed and switches off the light and let himself and every one present there to sleep. After a long interval of days, everyone in the room enjoyed a sound slumber.

It is at the breakfast table; Dr. Ranrajan breaks his mourning mood and shares his idea of penance with his parents. Out of curiosity, the Parents ask him how he is going to have it. He replies very jubilantly by adopting the boy of the departed patient. Parents raise their eyebrows which indicate their unapproved state of mind. His father tries to convince him that there is nothing wrong in spreading an umbrella of affection and care over an orphan boy but it can put all of us in trouble; the reason is that we are looking forward for your marriage. He says, "You have reached to a marriageable age. Parties of bridegroom are knocking at the door every now and then. If you adopt the boy what the families of the girls will think. I am afraid it will enhance our worries. It is my advice to you to think twice before you jump."

Dr. Rangrajan's sense of commitment to the welfare of the boy overpowers the doubts and concerns of the Parents. Any how he conveys the confirmation of his decision to his parents anticipating that they will not be agreeing with his going. One day early morning, he goes to the hospital and collects the address of the maternal uncle of the boy recorded at the registration counter. Luckily the bereaved family stays in the same town. With great efforts he reaches to the house of the boy. He finds that the main gate of the house is half open. He tries to have glimpse of the inner world through a thief's peeping. Surprisingly, he finds that the little boy is enjoying a swing and identifies him to be Rohan. Coincidentally, their eyes meet each other, the little boy bit scared hurriedly jumps down from the swing and runs into the house shouting "Uncle! Uncle! A new uncle has come and waiting for you at the gate. Let us hurry up." Uncle gets curious and comes out with the speed of Rohan. He gets shocked to see Dr. Rangrajan is waiting there hesitating to enter with prior consent. Rohan's uncle takes him in and does all possible hospitality.

They have a cup of tea and then flourish their discussion. Dr. Rangrajan opens his mind and confesses without any hesitation and fear of consequences of what uncle will think that it is because of his unskilled hands, Rohan lost his mother. Dr. Rangrajan anticipates that after listening to the confession, Uncle may get lose his temper or attack on him with sharp weapons of abuses but happens completely contrary. The confession fails to create that adverse impact. Uncle gets neither shaken nor annoyed. Uncle puts his hand on the doctor's shoulder as if he is supporting him. He tells Dr. Rangrajan that no doctor is that much flint hearted to do harm to the life of his patient who submits himself with great trust. He always sees and takes care that life of the patient should remain secure in his hands and no harm should be done to him. But sometimes doctors knowingly or unknowingly make such mistakes as if destiny wants him to do it so that blame should not go on her and cause the occurrence of something good to the sufferer. He tells Dr. Rangrajan that they have taken it to be the game of the 'Destiny' and nothing else. He further adds that the family has gradually recovering from that severe whip of destiny. They being mature have accepted the reality of life and mention without fail, that little Rohan is still stuck to the memories of his dear departed mother. Every now and then he asks, "Will Mummy be back and when?" and cries loudly with missing sound I miss you mummy come back wherever you are. I am lonely in this crowded world." Hearing the words of Uncle, a human tear falls down from his eyes bathing long hungry little space. Both become emotional and try to support each other. Uncle asks his tongue to take rest. Seeing his tongue at rest, Dr. Rangrajan opens his mouth, "You may accept it or not but my conscience always whips me with a blame that I am responsible for the ruin of the lives of Rohan and his mother it makes me want to do penance by doing something good to Rohan." Taking a comma, Uncle asks, "How would you take a penance for what have you done?" Dr. Rangrajan releases a breath of relief consoling him that at least a question how has come from uncle. He tells the uncle that he wants to adopt Rohan. Listening to these philanthropic thought, uncle gets moved by his attitude and gives a smile of appreciation to the doctor and asks for some time as the separation of Rohan would be hurting and painful to them. The doctor asks him to take sufficient time for giving confirmation and requests him to inform him about the day to come to take Rohan with him.

With an optimistic hope, Dr. Rangrajan takes the leave of Rohan's Uncle with absolute assurance to come on the fixed day. Meanwhile Rohan's Uncle discusses the issue of adoption of Rohan with the family. Everyone in the family comes up with positive remark. Eventually uncle assures everyone in the family that even though he is going away, he is going not out of station. He will be with us sharing the same town. All agree and the discussion ends with positive note to go with the idea of Dr. Rangrajan. One day, Dr. Rangrajan receives a call of affirmation and invitation from Uncle when he is having tea with his doctor colleagues in the canteen of the hospital.

On the fixed day, Dr. Rangrajan reaches to the uncle's house. Before going he takes full care that the boy should come with him happily. For this he takes a lot of toys and chocolates with him. Here in the uncle's house, Rohan is prepared with a small bag. Dr. Rangrajan comes and hands over some toys and chocolates to Rohan which remove all barriers of identification and within no time Rohan becomes one with the doctor. Toys are a great weakness of all children. How can Rohan be an exception to that? Toys are great source of pleasure to children after their mother. Sometimes the attraction of toys overpowers the motherly affection and the children gets amused and get mingled in the world of toys that he for a short time becomes oblivion to his own mother. Rohan starts playing with the toys and forgets for some time what is happening around him. After enjoying the given hospitality, Dr. Rangrajan gets ready to return. Uncle looking at engrossed Rohan in the world of toys asks him to make him mentally prepared for his upcoming journey. "Rohan would you like to go to Dr. Uncle's house." Hearing this sound, Rohan bids farewell to his world of toys and asks his uncle with a great greed for more toys. "Will I get more toys there? If 'yes' I will." Dr. Rangrajan gets happy with magic which toys performed. Listening to this question of Rohan, Dr. Rangrajan tells him that he has kept lots of toys in the taxi. On hearing this, Rohan starts towards the taxi parked outside the gate. He becomes very happy with the toys and once again enters the world of toy. The taxi moves towards its destination marking a new beginning of the life of Rohan. When the taxi takes a long pause at the house of Rangarajan, on seeing the new house, Rohan curiously asks, "Doctor uncle where have you brought me?" Dr. Rangarajan replies, "My dear Rohan, this is my house and there are a lot of toys which are waiting for you." Rohan surprisingly and with ample rapture exclaims, "Oh! Yes!" to this the doctor nods his head positively. The attraction of the toys takes him into the Doctors bedroom. The glamour of toys' world in the bed room of the doctor begins to wipe out the memories of Rohan's world in his uncle's house. Gradually Rohan becomes one with the family. The doctor's family willingly or unwillingly welcomes Rohan and loves him as their own little son. But the parents are troubled with a question that is what about the marriage of the doctor.

One day morning, sharing breakfast with their son Dr. Rangrajan, the parents raise the question of his marriage. They try to convince him that they have accepted Rohan and now it is his turn to follow what they say. Dr. Rangrajan with his causal response says, "What they want him to follow him?" They ask him to marry. On this, he replies very silently that there is nothing wrong in getting married. But the question makes him restless is whether the girl will accept him with the child. To make him feel comfortable the parents assures him that they will find out such a girl who will have this sort of magnanimity. Search is going on one side and on the other side the doctor is busy in educating Rohan and handling his responsibility as a doctor. A long period of time passes but no such proposal comes to the Doctor. With the maturity of the passing time, the doctor attains maturity in terms of age. He becomes middle aged person. It is the age when the question of marriage rarely touches the heart of the people. Doctor gives up the hopes to marry and engages himself in his responsibilities. Rohan becomes a great source of amusement for the doctor. Much of the available time, the doctor spends with Rohan. Sitting together for study, going out for shopping and site seeing, playing different games and watching programs on television are the some of the activities which they do together which strengthen their relation and they behave as if they are very close friends.

Doctor's parents disappointed at heart due their failure in finding out the suitable bridegroom for their lonely son express their desire to go on pilgrimage. Doctor takes no objection and happily arranges a travels which take the people on pilgrimage. The day of pilgrimage comes; the doctor comes to see his parents off at the place where the travels is parked. Their pilgrimage begins and doctor rejoins his world with Rohan.

One day, it is early in the morning that doctor receives an ominous call informing that the boat which carrying the pilgrims including his parents to a spiritual place is carried away by the flood water. He tells him further that efforts are in full swing but it is not found yet. He expresses fear that the horrible and terrific flood might have taken their lives. Voice of the speaker becomes silent by bringing permanent silence in the life of Dr. Rangrajan. It is a great shock to him and he takes a lot of time to come out of this mishap to parents. But he never allowed his personal concern to disturb his world with Rohan. Rohan has become enough mature to understand the upsetting things ruling the doctor's mind. The absence of the parents is missed a lot. It makes the whole house a treasure of sweet and painful memories in which the doctor's life gets drowned. A big house but only two are there to live. Absence of the both at house makes it a troubled heart dying for human presence. When both the Doctor and Rohan return home the house breaks his silence and becomes noisy as if he is giving an outlet to his feeling after a long interval.

Rohan's study is in a full swing. He is in the last semester of civil engineering. Dr. Rangrajan is happy and satisfied with a thought that he could do something for the sake of a mother who lost her life on account his mischievous fingers. The doctor's concern of Rohan's education comes to an end with his scintillating success in the final year examination. End of a concern is the beginning of the other. Now, Dr. Rangrajan is concerned about his marriage and job. Luckily, Rohan gets job as an engineer in Pune. It is good news for both but Rohan is disappointed at heart as he has to go away to a distant place leaving his father alone at home. Dr. Rangrajan does not want that he should lose job opportunity. He encourages him to accept the offer without bothering about their separation. Finally Rohan obeys his father and accepts the offer. The day of joining is approaching with enhancing the feel of unease for both. The joining day finally comes and Dr. Rangrajan comes to see him off at the railway station. There is time to arrive the train. Meanwhile Dr. Rangrajan gives him necessary instructions to which Rohan nods positively. They are so engaged in their conversation that they don't understand when the train arrived on the platform and blowing the whistle of departure. Both reach to Rohan's reserved compartment. They look at each other and with flood of tears in their eyes they embrace each other as if it is going to be their last meet. The doctor says, "My dear! You are going away. Be careful as there is no one of our acquaintance. Do well in your job and have nice relationship with everyone and make a nice friend circle so that you won't be troubled by the feel of isolation and my memory." Rohan stores all these words of fatherly affection and care in his mind and assures him, "Don't worry Pappa. I will do as you say." Rohan further says, "Dear Pappa, Promise me that you will take care of yourself and ring me before going to bed every day." To this, Dr. Rangrajan replies positively. Before getting down from the train he embraces him once again and once again their faces get drowned into the flood of tears. The train gives final blow of the whistle and leaves the platform. Both get engrossed in catching each other's view with running train. Dr. Rangrajan fixes his eyes at the compartment of Rohan till the train goes away until it looks like a vanishing full stop.

Dr. Rangrajan continues his routine with giving a call to his loving Rohan. There in Pune, Rohan with his talent climbs the ladder of success and grabs the best place in the book of management. Considering his job capabilities, the management decides to send him overseas to expand the roots and market of the company. He gives this news to Dr. Rangrajan during a phone call and promises to see him soon. While treating a patient, Dr. Rangrajan gets affected by the virus of an incurable disease which corrodes him inwardly and steals his strength. The body of Dr. Rangrajan has become too weak within to overcome this hazardous concern. One day Rohan comes to see Dr. Rangrajan. At this time he is alone. He is accompanied by a girl to whom he introduces as his beloved and tells him his plan to marry her before going to overseas. Rohan also adds that the girl is Jayshree works with him in the same company and she is also one of the members of the team selected for overseas project. Dr. Rangrajan becomes happy with his decision. The date of their marriage is fixed and they decide to make it court marriage. On the fixed day the marriage is performed and the couple prepares for their overseas project. Before going overseas, the couple comes to stay with Dr. Rangrajan. It is during their a few days stay, the couple comes to know about the doctor's incurable disease and its contagious nature. When Jayshree comes to know about this disease and its infectious nature, she becomes obnoxious and protective. One day Jayshree asks Rohan that it will be in their advantage to be away from the diseased Dr. Rangrajan. But being a son, Rohan cannot do so. But consistent hammering of it on the part of Jayshree, Rohan comes under her loving and charming spell. One day putting an excuse of going overseas, the couple frees themselves from the diseased company of Dr. Rangrajan and goes over seas.

Dr. Rangrajan is not at all hurt by the conduct of Jayshree but his heart feels sad at the sudden change taken place in his son. With the departing, old and decayed time, Dr. Rangrajan grows old and his decayed body has become so thin and weak within that he stops going out and prefers to confine himself in his bed-room. There is a neighbor, Mr. Somayya, who comes to talk to Dr. Rangrajan whenever he has leisure. They spend hours sitting on the chairs kept in varanda of the house. One day Somayya comes to see Dr. Rangrajan. During their talk, Dr. Rangrajan tells him that he tried a number of times to call his son but he could not connect himself with his Rohan. He asks Somayya, "Will you do a mercy on me?" Somayya gets hurt by the formal tone of Dr. Rangrajan and somewhat irritatingly replies to Dr. Rangrajan, "What nonsense you are talking about? Your formal tone hurts me and makes me feel that I am still dissociated with you." Coming to the point he says, "what can this dissociated fellow do for you?" Feeling a little bit awkward, Dr. Rangrajan says to him, "I wish to have the last words with my son, if possible connect me with my son Rohan who is overseas." Spending not a single moment, Somayya takes out his cell phone makes a call. It is received by Rohan's wife Jayshree. Seeing a new number, she enquires about it. Somayya tells her that he is the neighbor and friend of Rangrajan and tells her that condition of Dr. Rangrajan is deteriorating day by day and he wishes to have a talk with his son, Rohan. Hearing the name of Rangrajan, Jayshree speaks in an avoiding language that Rohan is out of station regarding his official work and may take some days to come and without asking about the health of Dr. Rangrajan she cuts the phone. Somayya understands the indifferent mood of Jayshree. Before he opens his mouth to tell, Dr. Rangrajan already has face reading during his talk with Jayshree and tells him that he doesn't want to hear the response. Somayya holds his hands and reads the feel of frustration and futility hidden between dark lines of furrows on his forehead. They finish their final talk. Before departing Somayya consoles him that there is nothing to worry. Things will be ok at their right time. Somayya leaves with a promising word that he will be back soon as he is going out of station for his mission. For the last several days he has not been to Dr. Rangrajan as he was out of station. In his absence, one day at the stroke of the midnight hour, the bedroom light gets off due to power failure. Dr. Rangrajan supporting his weakened body gets down from the troubled cot to burn the candle to kill the darkness but suddenly a puff of air comes and extinguishes the burning match stick. Suddenly Dr. Rangrajan falls down on the ground and never wakes up then. For several days his dead body remains in the locked bedroom. One day morning, Mr Somyya comes to see him and finds that the chair on which Dr. Rangrajan used to sit and welcome him is vacant and his bedroom is locked from inside. When he goes very close to the door, he smells an odor coming from inside. He takes the vacant chair stands to have a look inside. Suddenly he gets shocked to see that Rangrajan laying on the ground. As he becomes suspicious of the things inside, he calls the neighbor and with their support he breaks the door. When they go in their noses die for fresh air.

Immediately, Sommaya makes a call to Rohan, "Hello! This is Sommaya a neighbor of Dr. Rangrajan." Rohan little bit confused by the unexpected call of a stranger enquires, "What is the matter? What makes you to call me at this odd hour of the night?" Without wasting his breath Somayya says, "Rohan, your father is no more! will you come to do the funeral formalities." Rohan gives his cool and indifferent response as if he has cut off his relation with the departed one. "Sorry! Uncle I am so busy that I won't find time to come back. If possible finish the funeral formalities without unnecessarily waiting for me." On hearing this, Somayya feels broken at heart blames the growing inhumanity in human relationship. As a friend, he does all the funeral rituals. An unfulfilled soul of Dr. Rangrajan moves on a journey of fulfillment.

Shortening Lives and Growing Concerns

The early hour of the morning brings ample rapture to the little family of Devdhar, a poor peasant serving ceaselessly on ever infertile land in the village of Devgad. This morning hour becomes the most memorable in his life as it gifts him with a baby boy. Since the arrival of a new baby boy in his dilapidated hut, all seem to be singing a song of happiness in unhappy conditions. Devdhar wants to celebrate the arrival of the new baby but he is unable to do as he can not afford the expenses of celebration. He lives in such a hut where it becomes difficult to identify which is kitchen and which one is bedroom. His hut is so dark as if the light has cursed it of his eternal absence. It is in this disappearing and drowning darkness, Devdhar tries to struggle to take out a steel box which contains a little sugar. One catches his struggling stature in that darkness because he is in white clothing. So he conveys his happiness of getting a son by distributing that a little sugar. The crowd of people is seen for the next few days to be with them in their happiness.

Devdhar owns five acres of land which seems to be cursed with infertility. Irregular rainfall adds to the troubles of the village. Every year, he sows in his farm but nothing comes out of it which drowns his family in never ending poverty. Every year he takes loan from the landlords with the promise that he would return it with interest after coming harvest. But promise remains promise and harvest becomes a forlorn hope for Devdhar. Every barren year goes on adding a layer after a layer to the never ending loan taken by Devdhar. Sometimes poor rain steals his fortune or sometimes inability to get seed to be sown worsens the conditions of the family. Forgetting all these ever stored concerns, he arranges a naming ceremony which is attended by his very close people. They name the child Shridhar with hope that the arrival of the new baby would change the fortune of the dark hut. A short period of happiness comes to an end intensifying the growing concerns of the family. Never ending loan of the landlord and disloyalty of rain corrodes the entire family. Devdhar anyhow manages the expenses of the family by working on other's fields. Sometimes there is heavy rain which affects the harvest and sometimes the village dies for a drop of rain. These unpredictable climate conditions not only hamper the expecting harvest but also his hopes. In such a hopeless situation, he can do nothing but to be hopeful about the future. Thus the entire family grows on the medicine of hope.

Time passes with making Devdhar incapable enough to support the family in their worst conditions. Devdhar being completely frustrated with his unsuccessful life hands over the charges of worthless property and never ending load of landlord's debt to his growing son Shridhar. Since the family is not financially strong, there is no question of giving education to the only son, Shridhar. He takes the plough of the family on his weak shoulder as if he is newly bought ox.

frustrating conditions of the life affect the poor health of Devdhar who is already corroded by never ending concerns of life falls sick and confines himself in the bed. Since the time, Shridhar takes the charge of the family; there is a little improvement in the overall conditions of the family as if he is born to end the concerns of the family. Luckily every year there is sufficient rainfall which removes the infertility of the land. Shridhar earns good through his farming but most part of earnings is spent on the illness of his father and paying the debt of the landlord. For years, it continues but the concerns of ailing father and ever increasing debt of the landlord does not let him raise his head up. One day the ailing father expresses his last will to see him getting married. Since that moment when he attended the maturity, Shridhar feels that he has been leading for the sake of someone. Sometimes he leads for the sake of paying the debt of the landlord, sometimes for the sake of curing the ever ailing father but never has he got the chance to think of his life. The trap of the family concerns makes him restless. The more he wants to free himself, the more he gets entwined in it. For the sake of dying father, he gets ready to marry. The strange thing for him is that there is no one who can go in search of a suitable bridegroom for him. There is a mother who rarely finds time from her engagement in her ailing husband. She talks of Shridhar's marriage but very little she does to make it possible. So Shridhar with his colleagues finds out a girl for himself. The dying father is happy because happiness has returned to their door after long time. It had come when Shridhar was born in the darkness of the hut. It is self arranged marriage as much of the preparation of the marriage is done by

Shridhar himself and his friends. Shridhar gets married and brings the bridegroom home. Shridhar gets some money from the family of his wife as a dowry but it is too meager to perform this marriage. Much of it is spent on ornaments of the bridegroom and other things of the marriage. So the remaining money Shridhar manages in the form of loan from the landlord.

Shridhar's marriage throws the family into the valley of never ending concerns. For marriage he takes some money from the landlord which he takes years to repay. A few days after their marriage, the dying father takes last breath and frees himself from the cage of the never ending concerns and leaving behind what one calls inheritance of loss. Thus Shridhar loses his ever ailing support. Mother of Shridhar can not bear this separation from her husband and takes it to her heart. She falls ill and takes the place of her husband on the dying bed. Her illness continues for a long time which contributes to the adversity through which Shridhar goes. The entry of the new bridegroom is supposed to be a good omen as it brings good rainfall that year and good harvest for Shridhar. Shridhar is equally supported by his wife Shanti and their joined hands create miracles on the field. Harvest is more than expected that year which enables Shridhar to pay the loan with interest taken from the landlord. Good harvest of the year gives some relief to the concerned soul of Shridhar. It is on one night when the couple is resting on the bed, Shanti discloses the sweet secret, "My dear lord! If I give you the most mirthful news what will you give me in return?" On this Shridhar replies somewhat frustratingly, "My dear lady! I am neither the king to give you a kingdom nor a magician to bring down the beautiful Moon on the earth. Your husband is poor fellow but I promise you that I won't disappoint you. Don't stretch my curiosity open your lips, my dear lady!" Understanding the concerned life of her husband Shanti tries to convince him that she is thoroughly conscious of the financial conditions of her husband and she would not demand any such thing which would aggravate his concerns. She says, "I want neither the Kingdom nor the Moon on the earth. I don't have any attraction for such things. Give me whatever is possible for you." Without stretching the dialogue further she hurriedly tells him, "You are going to be father soon." There is no doubt that broken news takes him on the top of air. He slowly and carefully lifts her to show her that he is very happy. In a happy mood of happiness he promises her that he would give her something in return of this good news.

Shanti is sent to her parents' house for delivery. Meanwhile Shridhar toils and moils in his farm and there comes good rainfall to his help. Both create wonders. This harvest gives him more than expected. Through his earnings of the year, he renovates his ancestral cottage and purchases an acre of land from his neighboring farmer who is in urgent need of money. It is on the same day, he receives the news from the house of the wife that Shanti has given birth to a female child. On hearing this news, Shridhar exclaims in slow tone, "Goddess Lakshmi has entered the house!" So, he decides to name her first daughter as Lakshmi. He shares the news with his ailing mother. She also becomes very much happy as after a long time since the birth of Shridhar, the cry of the baby is going to be heard in their house. Shridhar is not destitute like his father to be troubled by the question how to celebrate the arrival of the new baby in their family. He distributes sweets to the entire village of Devgad. He arranges a feast for those who are close to his family. Thus Shridhar is fortunate enough to have such celebration.

A few months after, Shanti returns home which sinks the entire family in happiness. A grand naming ceremony is arranged to name the baby. Entire village is called for feast. Ailing mother sees the grand function and gets immensely impressed by the grand preparation and the way the occasion is celebrated. That night mother calls Shridhar, "My dear, Shridhar, my eyes are really fortunate to see such grand function which had never been there previously. It makes me feel proud of you. I am really very happy. I feel nothing is there to be achieved and seen. I will be happy and ready to go whenever death wants to take me with him." On hearing the word death he tries to shut her mouth with his palm and says, "What nonsense are you talking about on this happy moment? Don't worry you will live long." The crowd at the house starts dispersing. Shridhar finishes all the rest of the things and returns to bed where Shanti is sitting with her daughter Lakshmi. Shridhar opens the wooden cupboard and secretly takes out the documents of the purchased land. They get engaged in talk till late in the night. Before going to bed, Shridhar reminds her promise she has taken from him. "Have you become oblivion of the promise you have taken from me?" Shanti replies quite consciously, "No my dear Lord! How can I?" Shridhar takes out the documents from his pocket and hands over them to her and tells her, "My dear lady these documents are of our newly purchased land which I have purchased when you were away from me." On hearing the utterance of the land she becomes extremely happy and exclaims, "My dear lord! You have given me more than expected. I am really very much pleased with this."

A few years after the celebration, ailing mother takes her last breath which shakes the roots of the family for sometime. With her departure, departs the last memory of Shridhar's existence. Shridhar takes lots of time to come out of this shock. One day when the couple is engaged in chat, he opens his heart to Shanti that this time he wants a son from her. Shanti positively responds to this demand of her husband. A few months later Shanti is sent to parents' house for delivery.Little Lakshmi who is four years old accompanies her mother.

Mean time, Shridhar engages himself in farming activities. The end of the concern of the ailing mother marks the beginning of the other. When he is engaged in sowing the seeds, a stranger comes loudly calling his name. He is one of the relatives of Shanti. He tells him that he has come with good news of Shanti's new baby. Shridhar becomes eager and anticipates that it might be of a son but soon he gets disappointed and somewhat disheartened when the visitor tells him that for the second time, Shanti has given birth to a female child. What concerns him not is the coming of female child one after the other but the question how to get them married. Although he is concerned, he does not give up his hope to have a son for the family. It continues for five times and all the times he gets the same breaking news of female child. His family grows in size with five daughters with growing family grows his tensions and concerns also. Hard time and hardship re-enters in his life. Poor rainfall disturbs his smoothly going routine life. Growing concerns steal his sleep. Many nights he passes sleeplessly. He gets fed up with the way the indiscreet rainfall plays hide and seek game with him which enhances the families' difficulties in surviving in such uncertain conditions. There begins harvest not in the farm of Shridhar but at home as five daughters grow ceaselessly and attaining maturity and reaching marriageable ages.

In the last several years, due to scanty rainfall, Shridhar received nothing satisfactory from his land. His saving is not capable enough to perform the marriage of his first daughter and what eats him is the question how to perform the marriages of the remaining four daughters. Shridhar performs the marriage of his eldest daughter Lakshmi by giving in dowry from what he has stored in his account. The first marriage makes him financially bankrupt and makes him prosper in his concerns. Smooth life gets disturbed. All the time he seems to be engaged in thinking over the marriages of the remaining daughters. Till now he has been living for the sake of others and a question strikes to his mind how long this pattern of concerned life would continue and when he will be free from his regular concern to lead life for himself. Whenever he goes to the market to bring something for himself and his wife, the question of his five daughters troubles his mind. So he gives up the thought of buying for himself and his wife. He gives a pair of saris to his wife and a pair of dress for himself. Shridhar learns to limit his own and his wife's needs but never makes a compromise with needs of his daughters. He gives them all they wish and never lets question of money come in the way of fulfilling their needs. That is why all daughters are very happy with their loving parents. Shanti is a woman of greater understanding. She never complains for not fulfilling her needs. She is aware of the fact that how much a father has to bear who has to care five daughters. She is unhappy at heart as she could not give a son to Shridhar. Shridhar is equally good and never blames her for not giving a male child on the contrary he feels guilt of killing emotions of Shanti for the betterment of his five daughters. Thus a desire to live for himself and for his wife makes a permanent abode in one of the deep corners of his mind. He eagerly waits for that moment when he will be free from the concerns which steal pleasure from life.

It is on one night sharing bed with his wife Shanti, he gives an outlet to his innermost feelings. He says, "My dear lady! My whole life is spent in ending a concern and facing the new one. So far I have led for the sake of father, my mother and their concerns and now I have to live for the sake of daughters. The more I try to end the concerns, the more they grow in numbers. In thinking how to end them, I am losing my life and of course you also." He stops in the middle and after taking a brief pause as if he is fed up with these concerns of life says, "My dear lady! It is enough. I am really fed up with all these demands of routine life. I feel that I am losing my life in thinking about others. I am really unhappy at heart as I don't have any worth noting moment which I lived for myself. I am really in hurry to end these concerns of the life and lead a life for myself and of course for you. I always feel that I am guilty for killing my and of course your emotions of the desirable life." Realizing the intensity of the problems which he has to undergo in his daily life, she tries to assure him, "Don't worry my dear Lord! There is time for concerns and there is time of happiness. I am sure that very soon you will be free from the concerns of your life and lead the life which you desire for."

Indiscreet rainfall and infertility of the land betrays him very inhumanly. His feel of unease grows day by day. The question "how to marry remaining daughters corrodes and weakens him inwardly. At one time he thinks of borrowing loan from the landlord but soon he gives up the thought due to disloyalty of rainfall. So he finally decides that it would be better if he sells out the land. Shanti also takes no objection to his stand. He sells out four acres of land to get his three daughters married. Marriages are fixed and performed one after the other. Luckily all the girls get good husbands with well to do families. Shridhar feels little bit relaxed as the most of the worries are successfully overcome only the last is left and that is the marriage of his last daughter. The money he has secured by selling the land is almost finished over the marriages of the three daughters. He has just come out of the worry of the marriages of his three daughters and now one more concern stands before him which is how to manage the money for performing the marriage of the last daughter. He tries his best to gather the funds for marriage but no source supports him at this time. Eventually he makes up his mind to sell out the last piece of land which he has kept for the survival of his family. It is the piece of the land which he had taken from his neighbor. When he declares that he is kept the piece of the land on sell, one of the stranger comes and claims that the piece of land to be his own as a proof he produces the documents which state that the he is owner of the land and not the neighbor. Shridhar gets involved in contention with the neighbor for deceiving him. This is the most traumatic period for Shridhar as he has already weakened by the expenses over the marriages of the three daughters.

He becomes uneasy and finds no way to overcome the worry. He is really troubled with worries which occur in never ending sequence. He is fed up with it as it steals the pleasure of his life and do not let him think of himself. When Shanti comes to know about the dispute troubling Shridhar, she suggests him to take the matter to the court. Shridhar agrees but he is troubled with the fees to be paid to the advocate who would put and defend his side in the court. He goes to the landlord and borrows money which he pays to the advocate to carry on his case in the court. The case runs in the court for many months every day is a day of traumatic experience for Shridhar. The more he wants to come out of it, the more he gets involved in it. The night before the day of judgment Shridhar opens his troubled heart to his wife. "My dear lady I want to finish this business at the earliest as it troubles my soul very much. I fear that if the judgment of the court goes against us what would be our lot? We will be lost." Seeing her husband absolutely discouraged, she supports him saying, "My lord! You have never done wrong to anyone so far then how do you expect that God will do wrong to you. You stand for truth and it is my faith that truth always wins at the end. Don't worry tomorrow will be the most pleasant day in your life. Be calm and sleep thoughtlessly." These words of Shanti give him enough courage to continue his life till tomorrow.

The Day of Judgment comes finally and brings relief to him. The court declares that the claim of the stranger over the land which Shridhar owns now is absolutely justifiable and asks Shridhar to hand over the piece of land to the stranger as he is the real owner. The neighbor who deceived Shridhar is told to repay the money with interest to Shridhar within the period of fifteen days and on the charge of forgery; he will undergo two years rigorous imprisonment. Thus the judgment of the court gives him a great relief and he comes home hurriedly to share this news with his wife. Shanti feels extremely happy and exclaims, "God is there in his heaven and everything is right on the earth!" The judgment gives them a hope to carry on their troubled life. The neighbor follows the order of the court and hands over the said amount to Shridhar within the given deadline. Both are happy and get busy in preparing to end the last concern in their lives that is the marriage of their last daughter. As usual Shridhar finds out a good boy having good background for his last daughter. Marriage is fixed and performed on the day decided. During the period of marriage the couple is busy that they don't get the time think about each other. The house is crowded with guests, relatives and the people who have been very close to them. As soon as the marriage is performed the crowd of the guests starts vacating the house of Shridhar.

A moment comes when the couple is all alone giving each other the smile of happiness and satisfaction. Both are very happy as their worries are almost finished. Shridhar is happier than the later as the most awaited day is coming with the end of this night. The couple gets involved in a talk till late in the night. Before greeting good night to his wife, he says, "My dear lady! All the concerns have slept eternally in their beds. Tomorrow will be ours and only ours. We will not let our mind think of anyone else. Our concern-less life is knocking at the door. Get up early in the morning. I will take you for outing." With this optimistic note he greets Shanti good night and goes to bed permanently. But he forgets that all nights are not good. The next day morning Shanti gets up earlier than her regular schedule begins her morning to prepare for going to outing. She deliberately does not disturb his sleeping husband with a loving thought that the soul of her husband is really tired and she wants to give him rest for some more time. After finishing her responsibilities, she comes to bed and tries to wake him up but Shridhar does not respond. Realizing that her wish to give his soul a rest has come true but she complains that she had not expected a permanent rest for him. She cries loudly which awakens the entire village of Devgad. Soon she gets sunk in the edgeless ocean of concerns and embarks on the journey of shortening lives and growing concerns.

Disgraced Innocence

Animating morning has spread its fresh and colorful carpet on the town, Umapur. This hour of the morning observes a hustle and bustle everywhere in Umapur. People are making hurry to go to their works. Farmers along with a pair of ox are marching towards their fields. Old people are going to the temple to begin their day with the *darshan* of god in the temple. Children with their fresh uniforms are hurrying in queue to their schools. Housewives of the town are engaged in their household activities. A white python like smoke is going upward giving impression that something is set on fire. But going closer, it shows that it is not like that. It is the smoke coming out of a hearth where a woman is cooking in the veranda of a hut. A sound of dropping water comes out of the bathroom located in one of the corners of the hut. The man who is bathing in that decayed bathroom is Ramdas a chief security guard of the temple of Rangareshwara. The woman cooking on the hearth is his better half.

Temple of Rangareshwara is an ancient temple having glorious past of more than five hundred years. It is a temple of 'Lord Shiva' a very popular temple in and around places of Umapur. Devotees come from different places to worship this god and get blessings which they desired. Never ending queues of devotees are there on

Monday as it is observed as the day of Lord Shiva. What attracts the devotees is its ever shining golden pinnacle. A sheer look at this golden pinnacle gives a sense of satisfaction and reminds the devotees with its glorious past. All the devotees first take the *darshan* of this golden pinnacle and then go to Lord Rangareshwara.

It is in this temple of Rangareshwara, Ramdas serves as a chief security guard. He has been in this temple for more than fifteen years. His long service has always been known for its honesty, sincerity, commitment and selfless service done out of sheer innocence. Ramdas proves himself to be a great success on both the marital field and the field of work. At home he is a responsible, loving and dedicated father. Caring everyone's needs and sincerely leaves no stone unturned to fulfill the expectations of all his loving ones does not matter how difficult they may be. His sole aim is to keep his family happy with whatever he earns with whatever he has. As a security guard he does not earn much. His earning never crosses the meager amount of two thousand rupees per month. But Ramdas and his family have learnt to be happy in whatever Ramdas brings home. They have learnt to limit their dreams and desires with the limited income. Personally, Ramdas is very happy and satisfied person as he is happy with whatever he has and whatever will be there in the future. The whole family is tied with a thread of innocence.

On the front of duty, Ramdas is a great success. Everyone in the temple and in the town knows him for his honesty, sincerity, commitment and innocence with which he serves the temple for years. He never looks at his work as a duty but as worship of the temple. He is credulous, innocent and unaware of the ways of the life of the world. In every one he finds himself. As a sincere servant, he does all the fetching and carrying in the temple. He never distinguishes between small and big responsibilities. When temple is crowdless, he undertakes cleaning activities and makes the whole temple clean and fresh for the devotees. When it is crowded, he stands as a responsible officer making queues of the devotees and making darshan easy for all. He always takes care that disciplinary conditions would be maintained in the temple. Due to these qualities, he wins the trust of the management. Sometimes he goes to bank to deposit the huge earnings of the temple. When he is on night shift, he seems to be very alert and watchful. He takes a round in and around the temple to see any wrong thing should not happen. When the last devotee leaves the temple, he shuts all the doors of the temple. He checks out without fail that all the charity boxes and cupboards where the offerings of the devotees are kept. After switching off all unnecessary lights, he comes to his small cabin having an old chair and a table where he sits and takes nap assuring himself that everything is in proper order. During his long service in the temple, no incident of theft is recorded. The management is very much happy with the devoted service of Ramdas. Every year the management organizes a function in which Ramdas and his entire family is felicitated in front of the people of Umapur. This felicitation is a great accomplishment for Ramdas. He very eagerly waits for this day of the year as it boosts his morale and makes him serve the temple with greater passion. The family is also very much happy with Ramdas as a head of the family.

Things are going on very smoothly and suddenly an evil eye of the destiny falls on the happy life of Ramdas. One day Ramdas is on his night shift. As usual he takes all precautions and returns to cabin. Suddenly he falls asleep. A nightmare of theft in the temple steals his sleep. He suddenly wakes up and finds that his whole body has become sweaty and trembling. He hurriedly gets up and switches on all the lights and takes a round in the temple and gets relief after finding that everything is right and whatever he saw in the nightmare is false. After confirming the things, he comes to his cabin takes out a handkerchief wipes the sweat on his face and throws a serious look at the wrist watch and finds it is an early hour of the dawn. Perhaps Ramdas is oblivion of the superstition that dreams seen during the hours of dawn prove to be true.

The first ray of the sun falls on the temple and enlightens the whole temple with its light. Another security guard comes to relive Ramdas early in the morning. Ramdas goes home for rest. Temple is opened for the devotees. Suddenly a devotee comes shouting that the golden pinnacle of the temple has been disappeared. The security guard confirms it and instantly calls the Trustees and Police and narrates the whole incident. The news of the theft of the golden pinnacle of the temple of Rangareshwara spreads like a wild fire. Whole Umapur gathers in the temple of Rangareshwara. Devotees lose their temper as it hurts their religious faith. Ramdas is instantly called back to the temple. Police investigate Ramdas. Trustees lose their faith in Ramdas and declare him to be the culprit. The crowd gathered in the temple loses their control and starts shouting against Ramdas throws at him whatever they have. One of the angry men among crowd comes forward and demands a severe punishment for Ramdas. They blacken his face and place him on a donkey and take the procession through each and every corner of Umapur. During procession, the angry crowd throws mud on him and some spits on him and some become harsher by pelting stones at him. Ramdas is absolutely bewildered with the happenings. During his long tenure of service in the temple, he has seen lot of money and also deposited a lot of money in the bank. But never the shining of money or the thought of theft could corrupt his innocent mind and such a disgrace of theft on him makes him silent like a corpse. Crowd gets angrier and demands public death for Ramdas. Considering the uncontrolled situation, Police take Ramdas to Police Station for further investigation. Having not found concrete proofs of theft against Ramdas, Police release him.

A few days later, Ramdas returns to his hut. While returning to his hut he does not dare to have an eye with the people around. What hurts him is that it is place where he and his entire family were elevated and it is here he and his family have been disgraced. Ramdas enters the hut and finds that his wife is sewing tattered uniforms of her son. She looks at him and both embrace each other crying loudly and lamenting on their destiny. The family of Ramdas has full faith in him and discards the baseless allegations. In his absence, the family suffers a lot. Their children are expelled from the school as the parents of other children have objected to presence of children whose father is a thief. She tells him that the whole town has boycotted them and it is very difficult to survive in this situation as all the sources of income are ceased. They decide to leave Umapur.

After walking a few miles away from Umapur, they happen to meet a farmer who shows pity on them and gives them shelter on his farm. Ramdas carries with him the disgrace of theft throughout his life as Ashwathama carries a wound on his forehead till the time of eternity. The disgrace of theft troubles him a lot and makes him sleepless during night. The entire family of Ramdas works hard on the farm of the farmer and anyhow tries to survive in their adversity. Their earning is so meager that they cannot educate their children. A long period of twenty years is passed. His elder son Ramling becomes twenty five years old and Ramdas crosses his fifty.

Meanwhile, Ramling joins a jewelry shop as an artist in a nearby town and supports the family. His artistry makes him earn satisfactorily. The owner of the jewelry shop has ignorant of the past history of Ramling. If he had known that Ramling is the son of Ramdas, the chief security guard of Rangreshwara, he would not have taken him in his shop. The jewelry shop where Ramling works is a flourishing shop and it is always crowded with the customers. Ramling is always busy in completing the orders of the customers. Suddenly hard times come for jewelry market as there is an artificial dearth of gold in the market. The owner of the jewelry shop where Ramling works is very much troubled with consistent demands of the customer. He cannot break his word of completing the orders on time. He knows that if he fails at this time, the customers may show their back to his shop and feels fear that one day he will have to shut down his shop. He makes the market survey and finds that availability of gold is not possible for the next couple of months. He is troubled by the question how to overcome this worry and shut the mouths of the troubling customers? Suddenly an idea clicks in his mind. He hurriedly goes to the farmhouse and starts digging where there he had hidden a black colored bag a few years back. He takes out bag and finds some relief. The next morning he handovers the bag to Ramling and asks him to remove the copper quoting of the thing given. He moves head with affirmation. He slowly opens bag and takes the thing out. He finds that a heavy copper colored pinnacle is there. When he starts pouring acid on that copper colored pinnacle, the shining of the metal inside dazzles his eyes. He gets shocked because it is of gold. Ramling doubts that there is something wrong and doubts that thing might be accumulated out of theft. Suddenly he recalls the event which took place twenty years back. Without wasting a single moment, he hurriedly reaches to the police station and narrates the whole matter. The Police Inspector reopens the file. The police make a raid on the jewelry shop and arrest the owner along with that golden pinnacle. During investigation, the jeweler confesses that one of the trustees had sold it to him. Ramling and police reach Umapur along with the golden pinnacle. The news of finding of Pinnacle spreads like a wild fire all over Umapur. Entire Umapur and people from nearby places rush towards the temple of Rangareshwara. The goldsmith discloses the name of one of the trustees who had done this act of theft. When the police try to reach to real culprit, they come to know that the trustee recently passed away. The process of investigation gets stopped. Pinnacle is reinstalled on the temple. Police along with the trustees

Darshan

organize the gathering of people and appreciate the adventure of Ramling and confess the mistake which the police and trustees had made twenty years back. They call Ramdas and his family on the stage and declare him to be innocent. The whole Umapur laments on what they had done with Ramdas. They along with the trustees decide to do penance for what they had done with Ramdas. They call Ramdas and his family back to Umapur, offer him his lost service in the temple of Rangareshwara and a house to live at Umapur. The trustees call a chariot and ask the entire family of Ramdas to ride over the chariot. It becomes a huge procession which goes through each and every corner and lane of Umapur. The news of innocence of Ramdas spreads in Umapur and nearby places. Ramdas looks at his son shows him a smile of relief in his eyes. Gradually, procession gets dispersed. Ramdas along with his family returns to their home in Umapur. All are happy with the happenings. It is too late in the evening and all go to the bed. Ramdas is very happy and excited because tomorrow he would re-step in the temple of Rangareshwara after a long and unbearable exile. It is too late in the morning. Ramdas has not come out of his room. Ramling goes in the bedroom of Ramdas to wake him up and gets shocked to find that the soul of Ramdas is rested in peace.

Masterpiece

The first rays of the rising sun penetrate through heart of the darkness and make it wind up its existence. With the departing darkness, everyone in the village named Chitrakut escapes to take the sunbath from troubling cold of the winter which is just begun. The village is really beautifully located in the net of captivating hills. It is rich in all its aspects of the Nature. Looking at these aspects of the Nature, one may imagine that Nature in real sense exists here as if this little village is God gifted. The birds in the nest twitter loudly so that the entire Chitrakut would wake up and begin to work. The rivers, streams and the waterfalls which rested in the night begin flowing gently inviting the people of Chitrakut to enjoy swimming in them and their warm beauty. The rain has just departed making everyone smile. The fresh and lush green trees, the bush and plants and the dancing grass revitalized by the rain invite everyone in and out of Chitrakut to dance with them and sing a song of happy life. The green farms have compelled everyone to wear the ornament of smile. The sky is quite clear as the rain has shifted his colony of black veiled people which concealed his beautiful face from the world. It seems that the beautiful sky smiles at its own spotless beauty reflected in the gently flowing water of rivers and rivulets. The waterfall gently falls and flutters as if someone has hung a beautiful faint blue curtain at the top of the hill. Some birds take a huge flight in the air and spread happiness everywhere and inspire everyone to think to fly like them in the sky of never ending dreams. All these living aspects of the Nature make Chitrakut a breathtaking, lovely, cheery and riveting landscape inviting all the lovers of beauty to Chitrakut to mollify their senses ever hungry for delicious food. For the painters it provides constantly changing and rare landscapes for their beauty searching eyes. But despite of these natural wealth, Chitrakut leads an unknown life.

Being distant and geographically ill-located, the world and its inventions like electricity, schools and colleges are yet to rich there. The parents send their children to schools which are some kilometers away from Chitrakut. But the people of Chitrakut are happy with whatever they have and never blame God for what they don't have. The happy Nature has taught them to be happy in all the times. In such satisfied conditions, lives a family headed by a farmer Shivhar who earns sufficiently from his farming work. Shivhar has a son Ravi studying in the seventh standard. What makes him happy is going to school on foot and capturing as much beauty of nature as possible. Shivhar is very happy that his son Ravi is not bull-headed like him and has keen interest in books. He toils and moils to provide Ravi whatever he demands for his studies. Once it happens that Ravi is attending a drawing class. The drawing teacher asks his pupils to draw a landscape and color it. The teacher is taking a round and going close to everyone to see how everyone is performing. Suddenly the drawing teacher takes a pause at Ravi and gets so much impressed by his painting skills. The teacher moves his fingers through the curly hair of Ravi and gives a pat on his back. The painting is shown to everyone and the Headmaster comes up with special appreciation for Ravi which makes him feel on the top of the air. Thus the drawing class becomes his favorite class. Every day the painting of Ravi is displayed on the notice board which brings a lot of appreciation for Ravi. Looking at the captivating landscapes of Ravi, his drawing teacher predicts, "My loving Ravi, I am sure that one day you will shine on the canvas of the world of Painting." This appreciation and inspiration from the teacher enhances his inclination and interest in painting. Since then painting becomes his obsession.

Obsession for painting reaches at its zenith when he begins to find painting in everything around him. At home looking at the vegetables and their green and fresh colors, cattle grazing in meadows in an around the village, shepherd playing on flute and the beauty of the sunrise and sunset is always been his attraction and he promptly draws them. Sunday is special day for him. Ravi gets up early in the morning and reaches with his painting tools sometimes to waterfalls in the deep valley or sometimes at the greeneries at the river and rivulets. Thus he begins to communicate with nature and depicts its live and ever changing manifestation in his paintings. Gradually his skills bring him good name fame and recognition in his village. Of and on the neighbors and people in village come to Ravi with their request for drawing either of the portrait of their departed ancestors or some Gods like Ganesha. His father Shivhar becomes extremely happy to see that at an early age his son is growing with good name and fame in the town. But what worries him is the future in this field. He has seen many more summers in his life and knows that what future is there in the field of painting. He is wise enough to understand that the art of Painting either takes its artist to it's zenith of success or makes him an ordinary artist struggling to survive on his art. There is no doubt that Shivhar is happy at heart that his son is doing well but what strikes him is his excessive passion for art which diverts him from his academics.

Once he calls Ravi and advises him, he needs to study other subjects and doing painting whole day does not mean that he is studying. But Ravi ignores the words of advice of his father. Initially he keeps quiet but when the fever of painting goes overhead and seeing Ravi neglecting his academics, he shouts at him. "Ravi, I don't like you ignoring my advice. I advised you previously to concentrate on the study of other subjects but you continued with your interest. If you are looking at it as your career, I am sure that one day you would beg and then you would realize my words. Stitch in time saves nine. It is not too late, you begin the study of other subjects and side by side you continue your passion for painting. If you ignore it you would make us suffer and eventually you too." Ravi does not take it seriously and continues his passion for art. Whole day he gets engaged in the drawing this and drawing that.

On every Sunday, he leaves home early in the morning and visits various natural sites in his village. Sometimes he forgets to take his food as he gets drowned in his art. One day it is evening time, Ravi is drawing a sketch under the dim light of the lantern. Shivhar comes from the field and sees that his son is drawing some sketch. He gets irritated and snatches his pencil and drawing sheet. "You difficult child, why don't you listen to my advice. Your uncontrolled passion for this trivial art would make all of us beg. Stop your painting otherwise you will have to pay price for what you do." Shivhar takes away the pencil and drawing sheet and hands over to his wife warning her not to give it to the crazy son unless he asks her. Ravi wants to reply but seeing angry temper of his father, he prefers to be silent. Little Ravi gets frightened by this manifestation of angry father and the way he warned him. He determines that he would not touch the brush unless his father asks him.

In school, he stops attending drawing class and focuses on the study of the other subjects. Sudden change in Ravi disturbs his drawing teacher. One day at the time of interval, the drawing teacher calls Ravi in the staff room and asks him. "Ravi, what is wrong with you? I have been consistently recording your absence at the drawing class. What is the reason? Are you fed up with this art or any other reason is there which prevents you?" Ravi looks down as his eyes are turned watery and controlling the shading tears he says, "It is not the matter of my interest. I want to do it. I can't live without it also. But sir........." The teacher stops him in the middle and says, "If not yours then whose interest matters? On whose instruction are you going away from the art? Tell me who is he?" Ravi replies, "It's my father. He says that there is no future for me in painting. It would make them suffer one day." The drawing teacher gets shocked that such things are told to Ravi. The drawing teacher asks him to go. Meanwhile the drawing teacher meets the Headmaster of the school and conveys the whole matter. Both decide to meet Ravi's father.

The drawing teacher along with the Headmaster comes to Ravi's house to convince his father. When they come, Shivhar, Ravi's father, is working in his field which is at a calling distance from his house. When he gets the message from his wife, he hurriedly comes home and welcomes the guests. The Headmaster of the school says to Ravi's father, "We have come here to tell you that your son Ravi is an extraordinary artist. If he is given good exposure and freedom to go with his passion, we all are sure that one day he would be a star on the canvas of the world painting. We have realized his caliber and from our side we are doing all that we can to make him achieve his mission. We request you to give him enough freedom at home also so that the art within him will get bloomed. We assure you that his excessive interest in paintings won't affect his academics." Shivhar, the poor fellow just goes on listening what the Headmaster says and instead of retorting or questioning further; he prefers to keep mum and mixes his sound with them. The Headmaster and father's meeting makes the passage smooth for Ravi's passion for art.

The time goes ahead and with that Ravi also. He completes his matriculation and takes admission for art diploma in nearby city. His skills get further flourished there. Proper conditioning in Art College brings out a genius painter hidden in him. His painting skills make him very popular and thus he becomes the most promising student artist of the college. His ceaseless efforts at art bring out wonderful pieces of painting which he wants to display. With the permission of the

Principal of the college, once he organizes his own painting exhibition in his college. It is widely visited by the people of the city and most of the paintings are sold out on the spot. The exhibition gives him financial support and makes him realize that he possess caliber of an international artist. He sets the goal to be an artist of an international fame and creates wonderful masterpieces in art one after another. He successfully completes his diploma and aspires to go to Mumbai; the city which he thinks would complete his dreams. He goes home and tells his father about his achievements and expresses his desire to go to Mumbai for further study.

Shivahar is very happy watching his son climbing the ladder of success. He is ready to do anything and everything possible for such a hardworking and genius son. When Ravi expresses his desire to go to Mumbai for further studies in art of painting, without wasting a single moment, he gives him an oral consent and stands as a strong support in the way of fulfillment of his ambition. Ravi gets admitted in the topmost art college in Mumbai. It is the college visited by the world's best painters. Every now and then the renowned painter personalities visit the college and guide the students about the paintings. Watching their glory and their luxurious life, Ravi's passion to be like them gets aggravated. He draws outstanding pieces of painting one after another and excels all the students there and gets immense appreciation from all. Once the institute decides to organize a painting exhibition of its students. To inaugurate this, the world famous painter from Germany is invited. Ravi selects his two paintings which he thinks are very dear to his heart for the painting exhibition. The painting exhibition is inaugurated. Many artists all over India visit this painting exhibition with the intention that they would get the chance to have a talk with the world famous German painter. The guests are observing the paintings displayed and suddenly the world famous German painter takes a pause at the painting of Ravi and gets engrossed in it. The features of the painting are so outstanding that they steal the heart of the painter. All of a sudden he exclaims, "Marvelous! What a painting! What a combination of colors and effects are! What a presentation! I am really lost in seeing it. Who is this painter? Please call him here. I want to see him." The Principal of the college feels proud and instantly calls Ravi standing nearby. When Ravi comes there, the world famous German Painter gives him a warm handshake and embraces him as if two great painters represent two different ends of the universe are meeting. Looking at Ravi, he says, "My dear young artist, your painting has stolen my heart. You have colored it so nicely that it makes me kiss your lovely hands. I confess it that after a long period of interval, I have got a chance to see such painting which possesses the caliber of being world's classics in art." Ravi gets astonished with this appreciation and wants to say a lot but the stream of words gets blocked and with great difficulties he expresses his feelings of gratitude saying, "Thank You Sir. Thank you very much." The German Painter asks him to meet him after the exhibition.

When he goes to see him, he is having a cup of tea with the other guests in the Principal's cabin. He conveys his message through a peon to the artist. Meanwhile the other guests disperse and Ravi gets a chance to have free conversation with the German painter. He says, "Ravi, my dear young artist, watching your painting and its potential, I think you deserve to be an international artist. See, there is a world famous art gallery in France which invites paintings from the artists worldwide and announces the masterpiece of the art from them every year. I want you to send your paintings for that, I am sure you will rock." Ravi gets fascinated by the idea and instantly he conveys his agreement saying, "Sir, thank you very much for the confidence which have shown in my talent. I take your advice very seriously and soon I begin to work on that." The idea of displaying his painting in the world famous art gallery in France ignites his spirit. He determines that very soon he would begin to work on that ambitious project.

His higher education is going on very smoothly with new creative manifestations of art every day. One day the peon of the college hands over a letter to Ravi. He reads it and comes to know that his father is serious and wants to see him instantly. Ravi packs the bag and leaves for Chitrakut. He meets the father who is suffering from asthma. Ravi wants to take him to the doctor but Shivhar stops him saying that it is of no use now as the disease has crossed its limit. One day at the time of sunset, Shivhar feels difficult to breathe. Ravi sitting by him cannot bear this miserable condition of his father and prepares to shift him to the nearby hospital but before he does it, Shivhar takes the last breath. As a son he completes the ritual of cremation. The house is at mess as it is overcrowded with guests and the visitors.

Sudden departure of father makes him more responsible to himself and his lonely mother. The responsibility of looking after his lonely mother and farm falls on him. He feels frustrated at heart as he knows these domestic responsibilities won't take him to the desired high flight in the sky of art. His mother has grown physically weak now and is unable to handle the household and farming activities. She wants him to marry so that all things would be at their places. He aspires to be back and completes his education and the most cherished desire but the domestic responsibilities come in his way and thus he gets confined in Chitrakut. Now Chitrakut is not what it was. It is absolutely changed during this long interval. It is transformed into a town having all the facilities. The population has become double or more. As per mother's wish, he gets married and settles down in Chitrakut as a painter side by side looking after his ancestral farm. Soon he gets blessed with a son and names him Raviraj. His devotion and dedication to his profession makes him very popular as 'Painter Babu'. Everyone in Chitrakut fondly calls him "Painter Babu' which pleases him very much. He becomes a commercial painter fulfilling the painting needs of the people in and around Chitrakut. As the earnings from painting increase, he transforms his house into a sufficiently big house where he makes separate and capacious room for his business. There is always crowd of the visitors and customers. His popularity as the painter keeps him full day engaged. He is so busy in his profession and domestic responsibilities that he does not understand how years have slipped out of his hands.

Years pass like that of passing clouds in the sky. But he has not forgotten the enshrined desire to be an artist of international acclaim. It is still burning in one of the dark corners of his heart and waiting to be exposed. Ravi decides to work on his old project. He reserves an hour from his hectic schedule for fulfillment of his long cherished desire. After dinner, he goes in his room and shuts it down and begins to work on his painting to be sent for German gallery. One day his wife Seeta asks him about late night awakening. Then he shares his dream with his wife, "Seeta, I wanted to complete my education and be an artist of international fame. But sudden death of my father spoiled all my desires. I am working on a huge painting of a dancer which I want to send to the world famous art Gallery in France which invites paintings from the worldwide painters and announces a masterpiece from them. In addition to name, fame and recognition, it would give me prosperity" Seeta gets excited with the idea and says, "Go ahead Ravi. My best wishes are with you. Frankly ask if any support is required." Ravi thanks her and continues his work.

Raviraj his son now studying in tenth follows the footprints of his father. He also takes a keen interest in painting. Whenever he is free, he accompanies his father and keeps watching for hours how his father paints. Seeing his son's interest in painting, Ravi guides him and tells him all the minute things of this art. Ravi's fame as a painter crosses the frontiers of Chitrakut and he gets orders from nearby places. Whole day he is engaged in painting. He does not get time to eat. Sometimes he works with hungry stomach. When he finishes his day's orders, he moves towards his project and till late in the night, he works on that. The painting is about to be finished. With a long canvas, he covers the painting almost six to seven feet high. Whenever he goes out, he warns to his wife Seeta that none should touch the painting.

This hectic schedule has an adverse impact on his health. The burden of work so increases that he becomes incapable to complete the orders in time. It affects his health. One day in the morning, he takes the brush and is about to start day's orders of the customers, suddenly he finds that his right hand gets trembling and he falls down. Half of his body gets paralyzed. Raviraj takes him immediately to hospital with the help of the neighbours where the doctors declare that he has received a severe attack of paralysis and there is no chance of recovery. Paralysed Ravi is brought home. It is a great shock to the family. Seeta is almost collapsed but looking at young Raviraj, she controls herself. Now she is over burdened with responsibilities. She has to look after the farm, Ravi's mother and an ever sick husband and studying Raviraj also.

A cot is arranged in one of the rooms where Ravi has kept his painting project. Ravi feels sad over his condition and prefers to be silent. Whenever he looks at his wife, Seeta, tears start rolling down. One day Seeta is sitting beside Ravi and feeding him. Ravi begins to weep. Supporting him she says, "It is inevitable. We are helpless, when the things are not in our hands. In such inevitable and unacceptable circumstances what can you do? I think you should accept the things as they happen to you and learn to be happy with what you are and whatever you have. Learn to accept that you are disabled. If you don't, you will experience death at every moment of your life." These words of Seeta empower him and he breaks his silence. "Seeta, how much you have suffered on account of me. It hurts me. I feel that I have wronged you and Raviraj as well." Suddenly he takes a pause and his eyes are instantly shifted towards the curtain covering his dream painting. He says to Seeta, "What makes me unhappy is not my miserable plight but my unfulfilled dream to complete my dream painting." Once again he turns silent and gets engrossed in staring at the incomplete painting as if it is communicating something to him.

Once, Ravi is sleeping on the bed. His son Raviraj enters his room and silently tries to uncover the wooden frame and gets pleasantly shocked to see a beautiful incomplete painting of a dancer. He comes back to his mother asks her about the painting. Initially Seeta tries to avoid answering it as it is one of her bitter memories. But when she observes that her son has grown over obstinate and he is not in mood to accept negation, she breaks her silence over the incomplete painting. Listening to the things behind his unfulfilled dream, a desire to do something which would please his father begins to trouble him. When it is noon, he enters his father's room and finds that his father is engrossed in some deep thinking. He silently goes and sits beside his father and says, "Father, will you do me a favor?" Looking at his humble and ever obedient son who has never demanded anything and never complained about anything so far asks him, "Dear, what favour do you expect from me?" Raviraj feels free and opens the desire which is fluttering in his mind. "Father, I am not a great painter like you. But I have been observing you painting since my childhood. During these long years,

I have grasped the techniques and tactics which you apply in your paintings which make it a living one. Yesterday I saw the thing behind that curtain and mother told me about it which has caused a desire in my heart to please you by doing something worthwhile." Ravi somewhat surprised asks him, "Raviraj, my dear son, what pleasing thing do you want to do for me?" Seeing that his father has become soft, somewhat frank and in jolly mood, he puts his final question, "Will you do me a favor to complete your painting?" Ravi asks him, "How is it possible? How can you add the things which I want in my painting?" "Pappa, you just guide me. I will do exactly as you say. Trust me. I am sure that I can do it as you expect." Finding that his son has become obstinate and he is quite confident over his expectation, Ravi agrees to allow him to complete his unfinished painting.

The work begins. Raviraj colors the painting as his father guides. He cares that all the gestures and color effects would come in the painting. In month's time, turning nights into days, Raviraj completes the painting. Ravi sees the final painting and he finds himself in seventh heaven. He calls Raviraj and appreciates him kissing him number of times. In mood of joy and excitement, he calls his wife Seeta. She comes there. Ravi says to her," Seeta, see what has your son done. He has made my dream come true." Looking at the completed painting, Seeta gets astonished and exclaims, "Marvelous! Raviraj, you have done a miracle!" Raviraj feels very proud of himself as he made his father smile.

A few days later, he calls Raviraj and asks him to write a letter to the Principal of his Art College in

Mumbai inviting him here for some important work. Raviraj writes the letter as desired by his father and posts it. After some days the Principal comes to see him. They talk a lot as they are meeting after a long time. The Principal feels very sorry over the miserable plight of his most promising student. After having lunch, Ravi tells him the purpose of calling him here. He asks Raviraj to uncover the painting. Ravi does it and seeing the painting, Principal gets enthralled for some moments he stares at it and gets lost in its beauty. When he comes out of it, he says to Ravi. "Ravi, What a painting it is! Truly saying, I have never seen such painting in my life. It is really a masterpiece of art." Raviraj tells him in brief the story behind its completion which makes him give a pat on the back of Raviraj. Ravi humbly requests him, "Sir I want you to send my painting to France for the exhibition and I am sure that you won't say no. Principal says, "Ravi, you had been our most promising student. We feel very sorry over whatever happened with you. When you were fit you did a lot to enhance the repute of our college. As the Principal of the art college and as an artist, it becomes my prime concern to keep art alive and flourishing in all conditions and motivate the artists to take this art to its glory. Don't worry, Ravi. I assure you and it's my promise to you that your painting will go to France." Ravi feels on the top of the air with this superb affirmation.

Principal takes the painting with him and on the next day he sends the painting to France. The world's best art gallery has invited the paintings from the artists worldwide as per its years' tradition. The selection committee is there which consists of the world's best painters who shortlist the paintings. Out of the shortlisted, they chose one to be honored as the masterpiece in art of that year. The selection committee continues its short listing work of received paintings. One day the Principal receives a mail from the Art Gallery in France that his sent painting is shortlisted for the final round and very soon final round will be conducted which will choose the best among the shortlisted as the masterpiece and the news of it will be broadcast on T.V. on a particular day about which they will be informed very soon. The Principal becomes joyful conveys the message to Ravi. It is a surprise to Ravi and to his family. The Selection committee completes its process and honors' Ravi's painting as the masterpiece of the year. Immediately after the declaration of the result, The Principal receives the mail from France with coupons for free airline journey. At 8:00pm on the same, the news of the result of the masterpiece painting of the year is broadcast with the name of Ravi. The family of Ravi sitting at T.V gets astonished on watching the news. Ravi feels rejuvenated as his long cherished dream has come true. He calls Raviraj and embraces and says, "Raviraj, You made me happy." Raviraj feels overjoyed and silently receives the greetings.

The Principal calls Raviraj on phone and asks him to get ready to go to France for felicitation. The Principal comes to Chitrakut and takes the entire family to France. There felicitation program is organized in a huge auditorium which is replete with the lovers of arts and the audience all over the world. Ravi and his family is invited on the stage and honored and given a cheque of a huge amount. This is the most memorable and euphoric moment in their lives. Their eyes are pleased with warmth of happy tears rolling down on their cheeks. They all experience that their hearts beat faster as if they are dancing. The entire auditorium experiences severe vibrations caused due the huge clapping sound. The anchor of the program hands over the mike to Ravi to express his feelings. Ravi sitting on a chair holds the mike in his left hand. The flood of happily dancing tears block the outlet of his feelings. For a few moments, he silently holds the mike and silences his dancing tears. He begins his talk and narrates the whole story behind the completion of this masterpiece. The whole auditorium experiences the flood of tears in real sense. When Ravi ends the story and thanks to the art and organizers of the gallery which gives him this honour, the whole auditorium stands and gives him and his entire family a standing ovation. The clapping sound in the auditorium is long heard by the family which becomes their most cherished memory.

Printed in the United States
By Bookmasters